# TOEIC 900

## II

主編｜政大英文系 陳超明 教授

著者｜Stephanie Morris 及其工作團隊

# 目次

推薦序 好用就是王道 ————————————————————————— 5

TOEIC 900 導論 ————————————————————————————— 7

New TOEIC 測驗說明 ————————————————————————— 13

New TOEIC 題型範例 ————————————————————————— 17

本書分類說明 ————————————————————————————— 40

本書體例說明 ————————————————————————————— 41

## 句型解說及練習

## 🌐 Part A Texts 書信與公文

01. According to ＋ 資料、報導、人或機構 / 標準（根據……所說 / 按照）———— 46

02. whether ＋ S ＋ V（是否……）————————————————————— 48

03. contact/ reach/ connect ＋ 人 / 機構（聯繫；接觸 / 接通）——————— 50

04. 人 / 機構 / 事物 ＋ remind ＋ 人 ＋ that/ to-V/ of（提醒 / 想起）——— 52

05. 人 / 機構 ＋ am/ is/ was/ are/ were ＋ certain/ sure/ positive ＋ of/ that（確定）—— 54

06. 人 / 機構 / 措施 ＋ ensure ＋ 情況 / that ＋ S ＋ V（確保……）——— 56

07. 人 / 事物 ＋ be supposed to ＋ V（應該）———————————————— 58

08. 建築 / 設備 / 場所 ＋ be located/ situated ＋ in ＋ 位置（位於）——— 60

09. 人 / 機構 ＋ report ＋ 事件（報告；舉發；描述）———————————— 62

10. 人 / 機構 ＋ award ＋ 人 / 機構 ＋ 事物（授予；給予）—————————— 64

## 🌐 Part B  Persons 人際溝通

01. 人 / 機構 ＋ **communicate/ negotiate** ＋ **with** ＋ 人 / 機構（溝通 / 協商）——— 68

02. **it**/ 事物 ＋ **occur to/ happen to**（想到…… / 發生……）——— 70

03. **It** ＋ **is/ was/ would be** ＋ **a pleasure/ pity/ shame** ＋ **to V** / **that** 子句（樂事 / 憾事）——— 72

04. 人 / 機構 ＋ **apologize** ＋ **to** 人 ＋ **for** 事物（因某事對某人感到抱歉）——— 74

05. 人 / 機構 ＋ **file** ＋ **a complaint/ lawsuit/ claim** ＋ **against** 人或機構 / **for** 理由

　　（對……提出抱怨 / 訴訟 / 要求）——— 76

06. **rather than**（而不是……）——— 78

07. **would rather/ would prefer to** ＋ **V**（寧願做某事）——— 80

08. 人 / 機構 ＋ **accept/ approve** ＋ 人 / 事物（接受 / 認可）——— 82

09. 人 / 機構 / 提案 ＋ **recommend/ suggest** ＋ **V-ing/ that**（建議事項）——— 84

10. 人 ＋ **attend/ join/ participate in** ＋ 會議 / 團體 / 活動（出席 / 加入 / 參與）——— 86

## 🌐 Part C  Objects or Events 事物說明

01. 人 / 事物 / 機構 ＋ **prevent/ keep/ stop** ＋ 人 / 事物 ＋ **from V-ing**（阻止；妨礙）——— 90

02. **S** ＋ **V** ＋ **instead of/ in place of** ＋ 人 / 事物 / **V-ing**（取代；代替）——— 92

03. 人 1 / 事物 1 ＋ **replace** ＋ 人 2 / 事物 2（1 取代或替換 2）——— 94

04. **an alternative to** ＋ 事物（對某事物的替代品或方案）——— 96

05. 人 / 事物 ＋ **seem/ appear/ look** ＋ 修飾人或事物的字詞（看起來；似乎）——— 98

06. **describe/ treat/ regard** ＋ 人 / 事物 ＋ **as**（形容為 / 看待；視為……）——— 100

07. **access to** ＋ 設施 / 資源 / 場所（進入；進入的權利 / 通道）——— 102

08. 人 / 事件 ＋ **place/ put** ＋ 人 / 機構 ＋ **under/ into/ out of** ＋ 情況（置於……處境）——— 104

09. **S₁** ＋ **V₁, unless** ＋ **S₂** ＋ **V₂**（除非……）——— 106

10. 主要說明或訊息 ＋ **as well as** ＋ 附加說明或訊息（除了……還 / 不但……而且）——— 108

**11.** 人 / 機構 ＋ **provide** ＋ 事物 / 服務（提供……） —————————— 110

**12. There is no doubt/ question/ evidence ＋ that ＋ S ＋ V**（無庸置疑／無證據顯示……）— 112

🌐 **Part D Operations 商務運作**

**01. There is a possibility ＋ that/ of/ to V**（有……可能性） —————————— 116

**02.** 人 / 機構 ＋ **am/ is/ are/ was/ were ＋ committed to ＋** 事物 / **V-ing**（致力於某事）— 118

**03. In order to ＋ V, S ＋ V**（為了什麼目的……） —————————————— 120

**04. the aim/ intention/ purpose ＋ is/ was ＋ to V**（目的是做……） ————————— 122

**05. charge ＋**費用＋ **on sth. / charge ＋**人＋ **for sth.**（記帳／索價） ————————— 124

**06.** 人 / 機構 ＋ **launch/ start/ introduce ＋** 產品 / 事業 / 活動（開啟／開創／引進） —— 126

**07. S ＋ stay/ remain/ keep ＋** 修飾或形容主詞的字詞（保持；仍是） ————————— 128

**08. due to ＋** 原因（由於某原因） ———————————————————— 130

**09. S ＋ V ＋ because of/ owing to/ thanks to ＋** 原因（由於／幸好……） ——————— 132

**10.** 人 / 機構 ＋ **attribute** 結果 ＋ **to** 原因（歸因於……） ———————————— 134

**11.** 原因 ＋ **result in/ lead to ＋** 結果（促成／導致） ————————————— 136

**12.** 原因 ＋ **account for/ explain ＋** 結果（說明／解釋） ———————————— 138

**13.** 人 / 事物 ＋ **become/ grow/ turn ＋** 形容字詞（變成；成為） ————————— 140

題解

🌐 **Part A  Texts** 書信與公文 ————————————————————— 145

🌐 **Part B  Persons** 人際溝通 ————————————————————— 177

🌐 **Part C  Objects or Events** 事物說明 ——————————————————— 207

🌐 **Part D  Operations** 商務運作 ————————————————————— 243

索引 ————————————————————————————————— 282

# 推薦序　好用就是王道

　　出社會以來，我都在外商公司服務，一直需要用到英文，同事常常笑我說，我的常用句只有一百句。事實上我確實愛用我有把握的慣用句，可是直到看到這本書的內容，才發現好用的句法就是王道。

　　本書作者 Stephanie Morris 現任美商 Lynx Publishing Company EIL 系列大專教科書主編，在到出版社擔任編輯之前，她曾在 ETS 台灣代表處工作，擔任線上寫作產品（Criterion）的產品主管，並協助 TOEIC 的教學資料的編寫，並實際擔任公司英語訓練課程的講師，所以對多益測驗與英語教學都有深入的了解。她常跟我說，有機會要寫一本多益常用句法的書，沒想到這些好用的句法就這樣出現在聯合報上，現在變成了一本好用的書了。

　　這次 Stephanie Morris 及其工作團隊應《一生必學的英文系列叢書》主編陳超明教授的邀請，寫出以 TOEIC 常用句法（syntax）與用法（usage）為核心的書，依其對多益測驗常用的句法理解，整理出 90 句多益常用句法，讓大家能更清楚地掌握工作與生活中對常用句法以及使用的例句，只要用熟了，就可以在國際職場中輕鬆地使用英文了。

　　這不僅是提升多益分數的書，更是強化職場英文能力的書。本書以職場導向為主，談的不是題型分析，而是深入解析職場英文的用法，進而瞭解考試的內容與方式。市面上的多益書，大都以單字文法或模擬試題為主，但是誠如我們一直強調的，如果真正英語力沒有提升，沒有真正掌握職場英文的內涵，多益分數是不會有顯著的提升！本書不同於坊間的多益書，特別強調職場英文的能力提升，大幅增加考生的多益分數。此書內容在聯合報專欄連載時，獲得廣大迴響，不少高中職及大學老師，利用所提供

的內容，作為教學題材，集結成書後，更有利於系統式的學習。

聯經出版社《一生必學英文系列》叢書主編、國立政治大學英語系教授陳超明老師，近年來在英語學習及英語教學上帶動了一股迥異於過往的英語教育新思維、新觀念，他主張應該學習實用英文、有用文法為主，並加強練習及進入生活工作層次。Stephanie 所編寫的《TOEIC 900》系列常用句法正是呼應陳超明教授的一貫主張。

《TOEIC 900》系列，不僅能讓大家學習並熟悉常用句法，也同時可以學習到常用單字。最後，我要強調「好用且常用就是王道啊」！就像學國術，師傅一定先教你些基本套路，讓你熟用幾式套招，這樣出門應敵，就算不能打贏，也可應付一下場面；同樣地，熟用語法，自然會使你的英語溝通能力大為提升，《TOEIC 900》系列就是幫你打下深厚的多益國際溝通英文的底子，教你多益考試的基本套路！在此，極力推薦。

ETS TOEIC. 台灣區代表

王星威

# TOEIC 900 導論

　　《一生必學的英文系列叢書》強調的是從真實生活或是實作經驗中去學習英文，以目標管理的概念來規劃自己的學習內容與形式。也就是以生活中的語料去發展自己的語言學習原則。一些不實用、真實生活不會出現的，或是在國際溝通英文中不存在的，就不納入學習的範疇之中。過去我們出版了《一生必學的英文文法》、《一生必學的英文單字》都是依照這個原則。其中《一生必學的英文單字》系列書中納入的單字，是以職場或日常生活中實際有用的英文單字為主，從國際溝通的情境入門，掌握實用的英文單字。

## 為何是多益測驗？

　　《一生必學的測驗系列 — TOEIC 900》延續這個語用的原則，從目的性及目標性來規劃職場考試的學習架構。我們選用多益英語作為編寫方向，一方面是因為多益英語是職場實用的英語，也是國際溝通英語（English for International Communication）。透過多益測驗的能力提升，可以真正地學會國際競爭中所需的英文能力。此外，以真實工作、生活 real life 為主的多益測驗，提供的學習情境，對於學習國際溝通英語很有幫助。另一方面，因為在職場上很多公私立機構都使用多益作為工作晉升或進用人才的標準，所以藉著多益英語的正確學習概念，協助大家在多益考試上能有好成績，強化在職場上的國際溝通能力。

## 這不是一本解題的書，這是一本提升英語文能力的自學手冊！

不管是在多益測驗得高分或提升職場英文能力，都不應該將重點只放在做模擬試題的概念上。實際上，我們曾做過研究，如果不能真正地提升英語文能力，只強調解題技巧，多益分數是不會增加的！坊間的多益書籍都是著重練習題目、分析題型、背單字或分析文法，這些書籍對於語言能力的提升幫助不大，對分數的提升也很少超過50分的，都還在誤差範圍中。本書重點在提升學生能力，在學習架構的規劃上不是去假設多益考試會考什麼，而是透過很多的研究與蒐集，獲得多益英語真實情境的語言資料，從資料中做整體的分析，再把多益考試的情境帶到學習者面前來做有用的學習。

如同《一生必學的英文單字》系列，我們是先從真正的多益考試、真正的職場英語裡回推回來，讓學習者知道應該要學那些單字，找出大家真正應該學的基本國際溝通基本字彙，讓學習者學得應該具備的單字能力。在《一生必學的測驗系列 — TOEIC 900》中也是如此，我們先整理出國際溝通英文中的基本句法，讓大家透過這些句法的學習，強化國際溝通的英文能力。

## 練習句法，不談瑣碎的文法規則！

一般來說，很多語言學習的文法書，將文法著重於規範性語法（prescriptive grammar），強調文法結構上的規範性，也就是一定要照規則來，否則英文是錯誤的。但是強調功能性與目標性的多益英語，對文法的概念是著重於敘述性語法（descriptive grammar），主要是描述一個真實的語言現象，不是告訴你語言要怎麼講，而是告訴你要如何用。這種功能性的語法，才是這本書要強調的。

## 本書的理論架構：強調具功能性、溝通性的語法結構

至於為什麼重視句法（syntax）而不談文法？文法可以說是用來規範語文的規則，當然很重要。但是句法才是一個語言溝通中最重要的概念。也就是將英文的單字排列方式搞清楚後，知道哪些字要放在哪裡、哪些句法表達某些含義，這樣就可以掌握溝通的重要方式。多益考試絕對是強調溝通與語意的理解，而非一些規範性的傳統文法規則。

描述性的語法強調功能性、溝通性，所謂功能性指的是在國際溝通中或考試上、實務性上用得到的。功能性語法有兩個基本的概念，一是要學有用的語法，另一個是這個語法應是實際情境中用得到的，而非一般文法書上所提供的結構性的文法概念。比如說有些句子是在傳統文法書上看起來好像不太對，但是在實際溝通場合外國人就是這麼講，這就是功能性的，才是有用的文法。從溝通性、功能性的文法角度來看，只要語意上沒有錯，字的排列是正確的，對於語意上的溝通是沒有影響的。這就是本書以句法入門，提升英文能力的理論架構。

真正對語言學習過程中有影響的，一個是單字，一個是字的排列次序。因為要懂得單字的意思才能明白溝通的內容；另一個是字的位置要排對，這就牽涉到這本書裡談到的句法 syntax，因為句法就是告訴你字要怎麼排，要怎麼使用。

## 本書不出模擬試題，而是以提升能力為主！

或許會有人納悶為什麼《一生必學的測驗系列》為什麼不出模擬試題？這是因為模擬試題不是真實的題目，很多模擬試題與多益真正的職場情境差異過大，只是強調

一些瑣碎文法。從題目去練習題目，不是有意義的做法，這樣的方式只是在加強解題技巧。我們一再強調：如果語言能力沒有提升，解再多模擬試題也沒有用，因為多益不是一種靠解題技巧，而是以能力指標為主的測驗，不是一種練習技巧的測驗，不像是數學做題解題式的學習。因此，以模擬試題的型式來學習多益英語，是本末倒置，如果語文能力沒有提升，花再多時間做模擬試題都是白費力氣，因為多益不會重複出題，縱然單字一樣，題目也不一樣；做了太多模擬試題的練習反而會被誘答，你以為這題做過，其實題目是完全不一樣的，結果就答錯了。所以多益英語學習中最重要的是要提升語文能力，才能夠提升你的考試分數。而在多益英語的學習中，分數只是其中的目標之一，如果只著眼於分數，即便考了 8、9 百分的高分，若是進入到職場還是沒有用，那終究還是會被職場淘汰。因此多益英語的學習應著眼於語文能力的提升，相對的，考試成績也將提升。

## 本書的學習方法

《一生必學的測驗系列 — TOEIC 900》中，我們整理的句法，是屬於描述性、功能性的，刪除了很多與語意無關的文法概念，在國際溝通裡面一些瑣碎的文法如與功能性無關，就不列入《TOEIC 900》的句法。為什麼選擇這些句法，如何決定其句法 syntax 功能性在哪裡？決定句法 syntax 的有兩件事，一個是動詞用法，另一個是有意義的片語、語法結構或有意義的轉折語及功能語。這些句法都經過職場驗證，也經長久測試，確實出現在多益考題之中！

傳統上，我們說句型有 900 個，其實這種說法是強調例句的練習。真正實用的句法經過整理，縮減為 90 句左右，把類似的句法放在一起，如 refer to/ resort to，化繁

為簡，有利學習者靈活運用。

　　為什麼書名取名為《TOEIC 900》，意指書中整理出來的 90 句可以化成 900 句，讓使用者在語言的應用上更加的豐富，在國際溝通上暢行無礙；此外，挑戰多益 900 分，已經是跨國公司經理的重要目標，想要獲得高薪、想要晉身全球化高階人才，一定要藉著本書正確的學習，在多益測驗中考得 900 分以上，實現夢想！

## 如何運用這本書來做正確的學習

### 1. 熟悉用法
請注意句中影響語意的關鍵字詞、注意句子的動詞用法及注意句子的字序排列；比如說動詞後是加物還是人，動詞要不要加 ing，介系詞放哪裡等。

### 2. 細讀例句
看完句型說明，要看例句，因為例句是句型的實際運用，透過例句可以更強化對句法及語意的掌握。

### 3. 大聲誦讀
因為多益英語是國際溝通英語的學習，可能是在書寫電子郵件時出現，也可能是在簡報時會出現。不管是口語或書寫，聲音的效果很重要。透過聲音可以把文字的印象強化，畢竟語言就是一種聲音的呈現。沒有口語的練習，也就沒有溝通的可能。

## 4. 勤做練習

再好的學習內容，如果沒有透過自我練習，終究不會真正化為自己的能力，各位可以兩天練習一個句型，藉著練習提升國際溝通能力。

依照本書的學習架構依序學習，相信各位都可以在考試及職場上無往不利，成為國際溝通能力的強手！

國立政治大學英文系教授

陳超明

# New TOEIC 測驗說明

## TOEIC 簡介

TOEIC 測驗全名為 Test of English for International Communication，是專供母語非英語人士的英語能力測驗，測驗分數反映受測者在國際職場環境中的英語溝通能力。

TOEIC 並沒有所謂的「通過」或「不通過」，而是將受測者的能力，以聽力 5～495 分、閱讀 5～495 分、總分 10～990 分的分數來呈現，受測者可以由此得知現在的英語能力，也可以設定將來想達到的目標分數。

TOEIC 目前是全世界最大的職場英語能力測驗，在全世界 60 多個國家實施，擁有 8,000 個以上的超大型企業客戶，受測者一年約 450 萬人。TOEIC 不但在企業界被廣泛使用，作為英語培訓績效檢驗標準、員工招募、外派或駐外人員篩選標準及晉升要件，在校園中也常被用作英語課程分級輔助工具、英語課程學分認定評量，或入學及畢業的標準。

## 研發製作單位簡介

TOEIC 測驗是由美國教育測驗服務社 Educational Testing Service 所研發製作。ETS 是目前全球規模最大的一所非營利教育測驗及評量單位，專精教學評量和測驗心理學、教育政策的研究，在教學研究領域上居於領導地位。該機構擁有教育專家、語言學家、統計學家、心理學家等成員約 2,800 名，發展的測驗及語言學習產品包括 TOEFL、TOEIC、TOEIC Bridge、TSE、GRE、GMAT、SAT、Criterion 等。

## TOEIC 的革新

TOEIC 自 1979 年研發至今，已有超過 30 年的歷史，是全球最受歡迎的職場英語測驗。ETS 為了進一步提升 TOEIC 對於國際職場的價值及應用範圍，2008 年決定將測驗形式更新。這些變化對於在國際職場尋求成功的人士而言，能增加多益測驗的價值，也能幫助企業評估他們員工，是否擁有足夠的英語溝通能力。

多年來，ETS 持續在測驗與學習的品質及公正性上努力，這也使得 ETS 的評量工具，與現行的學習理論息息相關。現有的語言理論界定了現實語言的複雜性，在這樣的背景下，學習者需要使用多種學習工具，來理解所吸收的資訊；而在真實狀況的溝通下，通常會需要同時使用詞彙、文法、語音，以發揮真實的語言能力。ETS 希望能夠同時達到技術上及溝通上的正確性及有效性。

## More Authentic：更真實的測驗

New TOEIC 測驗包含更多更加寫實的英文閱讀與聽力題型。聽力測驗的改變包括了出題內容的增長、出題內容變換的減少（連鎖題組）、以及不同的英語腔調。而在閱讀方面，變化包括了出題內容的增長、挑錯題的去除，以及閱讀測驗的型態更新，以測量考生對多篇文章的關聯性理解。

聽力測驗原本的照片描述一共有 20 題，新 TOEIC 則縮減為 10 題；第三大題的簡短對話及第四大題的簡短獨白，加長了題目內容，減少了題目的題數，改為以題組的

方式測驗。這樣的新型態測驗，將能測驗考生的實際反應能力。此外，新 TOEIC 將包含四種不同的英語口音，題目中可能出現美式、英式、澳洲／紐西蘭式及加拿大式英語。因為 TOEIC 所要測驗的，就是國際間能運用的英語能力，因此考生有可能在實際生活中，面對多種的英語發音，如此做法也能反映出考生將來在國際職場上遇到的真實狀況。

　　閱讀測驗部分第一部分將維持不變，仍為填空，但第二部分的挑錯則刪除了，而改為短文克漏字選擇題，旨在測驗考生是否具有整合句子及段落意思的能力。另一項改變則是最後一部分的文章閱讀，為了測驗考生是否具有交叉閱讀一篇以上相關文章的能力，考生需閱讀兩篇文章（可能是 e-mail、廣告……等），並根據兩篇文章所提供的資訊，來回答問題。在改版後的閱讀測驗中，考生將有機會證明自己是否具備現實生活中實際應用的技巧。

## 原 TOEIC 測驗

| 單元 | 大題 | 內容 | | 題數 |
|------|------|------|------|------|
| 聽力測驗 | 1 | Photographs | 照片描述 | 20 題 |
| | 2 | Question-Response | 應答問題 | 30 題 |
| | 3 | Short Conversation | 簡短對話 | 30 組 30 題 |
| | 4 | Short Talks | 簡短獨白 | 約 10 組 20 題 |
| 閱讀測驗 | 5 | Incomplete Sentences | 填空 | 40 題 |
| | 6 | Error Recognition | 挑錯 | 20 題 |
| | 7 | Reading Comprehension | 閱讀測驗 | 約 15 組 40 題 |

## New TOEIC 測驗

| 單元 | 大題 | 內容 | | 題數 |
|---|---|---|---|---|
| 聽力測驗 | 1 | Photographs | 照片描述 | 10 題 |
| | 2 | Question-Response | 應答問題 | 30 題 |
| | 3 | Short Conversation | 簡短對話 | 10 組 30 題 |
| | 4 | Short Talks | 簡短獨白 | 10 組 20 題 |
| 閱讀測驗 | 5 | Incomplete Sentences | 填空 | 40 題 |
| | 6 | Text Completion ( 新 ) | 克漏字 | 3 組 12 題 |
| | 7 | Reading Comprehension | 閱讀測驗 · 單篇閱讀 · 雙篇閱讀 | · 7-10 組共 28 題 · 4 組 20 題 |

## TOEIC 計分方式

測驗分數由答對題數決定。將聽力及閱讀兩部分的答對題數，轉換成分數，範圍在 5 到 495 分之間。兩個單項分數加起來即為總分，範圍在 10 到 990 分之間。答錯不倒扣。

## 報名 TOEIC 測驗

網站：www.toeic.com.tw

電話：(02)2701- 8008

# New TOEIC 題型範例

　　TOEIC 的聽力單元分為四個大題，閱讀測驗分為三個大題，試題本上各大題開始處，都有英文的 Directions，內容為題型及答題說明，請依照說明來完成每個大題。

## 一般說明

實際測驗的試題本上印有以下指示，說明作答方式。

### General Directions

　　This test is designed to measure your English language ability. The test is divided into two sections: Listening and Reading.

　　You must mark all of your answers on the separate answer sheet. For each question, you should select the best answer from the answer choices given. Then, on your answer sheet, you should find the number of the question and fill in the space that corresponds to the letter of the answer that you have selected. If you decided to change an answer, completely erase your old answer and then mark your new answer.

## 中譯

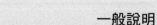

### 一般說明

本項測驗為英語能力評量測驗，測驗共分為聽力與閱讀兩部分。

請將全部答案畫記在答案卡上。回答問題時，請從選項中，挑選一個最適當的答案，並在答案卡上，將對應的選項圓圈塗滿畫黑。欲修正答案時，請將已畫記的答案擦拭乾淨，再重新畫記新的答案。

## 聽力測驗

### LISTENING TEST

In the Listening test, you will be asked to demonstrate how well you understand spoken English. The entire Listening test will last approximately 45 minutes. There are four parts, and directions are given for each part. You must mark your answers on the separate answer sheet. Do not write your answers in the test book.

# PART 1

**Directions** : For each question in this part, you will hear four statements about a picture in your test book. When you hear the statements, you must select the one statement that best describes what you see in the picture. Then find the number of the question on your answer sheet and mark your answer. The statements will not be printed in your test book and will be spoken only one time.

1.

🔵 中譯

## 聽力測驗

在聽力測驗中,請回答問題以測驗你英文聽力的能力。完整的聽力測驗長約 45 分鐘。共有四部分,每一部分將有作答說明。請在答案紙上畫記你的答案。請勿在試題本上書寫答案。

說明：在這個部分的每個問題，你會聽到針對試題本每張圖片所做的四段描述。聽到選項後，請選擇將照片描述得最完整正確的答案，並將答案畫記在答案紙上。四段描述不會印在試題本上，每題只播放一次。

● 題解

## 1. 🎧

**聽力原文：**

(A) The boat is tied to the dock.

(B) The duck is swimming around the lake.

(C) The passengers are about to board the ferry.

(D) The people are diving into the water.

**原文翻譯：**

(A) 小艇栓在碼頭。

(B) 鴨子在湖中游來游去。

(C) 乘客即將搭渡船。

(D) 人們跳進水裡。

**答案：**(A) 小艇栓在碼頭。

**題解：**Boat 一般指像照片中那樣的「小型船」，tie 原意是「繫、栓」，dock「碼頭」。(B) duck「鴨子」的發音是 /dʌk/，與 (A) 的 dock /dɑk/（美語）或 /dɔk/（英語）類似，所以要注意。(C) passenger「乘客」，board 是動詞「搭～」，ferry「渡船」。(D) dive into ～「跳進～」，the water 為「水（中）、海（水）、河、湖」。

# Part 2

**Directions** : You will hear a question or statement and three responses spoken in English. They will be spoken only one time and will not be printed in your test book. Select the best response to the question or statement and mark the letter (A), (B), or (C) on your answer sheet.

**11.** Mark your answer on your answer sheet.

## 中譯

### PART 2：（應答問題 / 30 題）

說明：在這個部分，你會聽到一個問題以及三種不同的回答，問題及答案的三個選項都只播放一次，同時都不會印在試題本上，請針對聽到的內容選擇最適合的答案，在答案紙上畫記 (A)、(B) 或 (C)。

11. 請在答案紙上畫記答案

## 題解

**11.**

聽力原文：

What time do you get off work today?

(A) Three times.　　(B) Around 5:30.　　(C) All holidays.

## Part 3

**Directions**：You will hear some conversations between two people. You will be asked to answer three questions about what the speakers say in each conversation. Select the best response to each question and mark the letter (A), (B), (C), or (D) on your answer sheet. The conversations will be spoken only one time and will not be printed in your test book.

**41.** What are the speakers discussing?

(A) Their homes

(B) Their jobs

(C) Their travel plans

(D) Their favorite cities

**42.** What does the man want to do?

(A) Get a new job

(B) Visit another city

(C) Find a larger department

(D) Move to the country

**43.** What can be inferred about the woman?

   (A) Her house is very small.    (B) She thinks the city is exciting.

   (C) Her job is very difficult.    (D) She lives outside the city.

## 🌐 中譯

說明：在這個部分，你會聽到兩個人之間的簡短對話，每段對話對應三道與對話內容有關的試題，每題有四個選項，請從中選擇最適當的答案，並在答案紙上畫記 (A)、(B)、(C) 或 (D)。對話只播放一次，內容不會印在試題本上。

## 🌐 題解

# 41. - 43.

聽力原文：

W : How do you like your new apartment, James?

M : Well, I enjoy living downtown, but I don't like that my apartment is so small. I want to get a bigger one, but rent in the city is so expensive!

W : I think so, too—that's why I bought a place out of town. It takes me longer to get to work, but my house in the country has a lot more space.

原文翻譯：

女：James，新公寓如何？

男：嗯……住在市區是很好，但是我的公寓太小了，我不喜歡。我想要住更大一點的地方，但是市區的房租非常貴！

女：我也是這麼想的，所以我才買市郊的房子，雖常通勤時間長，但是郊外房子的空間大多了。

# 41. 🎧 ........................................................

答案：(A) 他們的家

中譯：兩人在談論什麼？

    (A) 他們的家           (B) 他們的工作

    (C) 他們的旅行計畫      (D) 他們喜歡的城市

題解：由 apartment、living、rent、house 等關鍵字，可以知道話題是在 homes「家」，apartment 是「公寓」。(B) 有關工作，女生只有在最後說到「通勤時間很長」。(C) 話題沒有提到旅行。(D) cities 雖然是「城市」，但是兩人並沒有提到喜歡哪個城市。

# 42. 🎧 ........................................................

答案：(C) 找間更大的公寓

中譯：男生希望做什麼？

    (A) 找新工作           (B) 到其他城市去

    (C) 找間更大的公寓      (D) 搬到郊外

題解：男生說到 I want to get a bigger one.「想要更大的」是引導答案的關鍵，one ＝ apartment。(A) 跟 (B) 是完全沒有提到的話題。(D) 雖然女生住在郊外，但是男生並沒有說他也這麼希望做。

# 43.

**答案：** (D) 她住在郊外。

**中譯：** 關於這位女士，可以做出何種推測？

    (A) 她的家非常小。        (B) 她覺得都市非常棒。

    (C) 她的工作非常困難。     (D) 她住在郊外。

**題解：** infer「推測」，答案在女士的第二句話中出現，由 I bought...town. 或 my house in the country 可判斷。(A) 家（公寓）很小是男士說的，女士說的是她的房子空間很大。(B) 跟 (C) 是完全沒有提到的話題。

## PART 4

**Directions :** You will hear some short talks given by a single speaker. You will be asked to answer three questions about what the speaker says in each short talk. Select the best response to each question and mark the letter (A), (B), (C), or (D) on your answer sheet. The talks will be spoken only one time and will not be printed in your test book.

**71.** Where is this announcement being made?

    (A) At a train station        (B) At a travel agent's office

    (C) At an airport            (D) At a coffee shop

**72.** What is the weather like in Hong Kong?

    (A) It is foggy.           (B) It is clear.

    (C) It is snowing lightly.     (D) It is stormy.

**73.** What time of day is this announcement being made?

    (A) Morning                            (B) Afternoon

    (C) Evening                            (D) Late night

🔘 中譯

> ### PART 4：（簡短獨白 / 30 題）
>
>     說明：在這個部分，你會聽到幾段簡短的獨白。每段獨白會對應兩～三道試題，每題有四個選項，請從中選擇最適當的答案，在答案紙上畫記 (A)、(B)、(C) 或 (D)。每段獨白只播放一次，內容不會印在試題本上。

🔘 題解

# 71. - 73.

> 聽力原文：
>
> Attention, Trans Air passengers. Due to unusually strong storms, flights from Hong Kong have been delayed. In addition, flights to or through Hong Kong will be unable to take off until the weather system clears. Please accept our apologies for any inconvenience this may cause you. If there is any way we can make your wait more comfortable, please let the gate agent know. In the meantime, we are pleased to offer all passengers a continental breakfast in the waiting area. The food will be available all morning. Please help yourself to coffee or tea, pastries,

and fruit. We will announce new flight schedules as they become available. For now, try to relax and be patient. Thank you, and have a good morning.

原文翻譯：

搭乘 Trans Air 的旅客們請注意，由香港出發的航班因為異常暴風雨的關係而延誤抵達時間，前往香港或經由香港的各班機預計在天候恢復之前無法起飛，造成各位的不便請見諒。在等候期間，若有任何可使您的等候更為舒適之處，請向門口服務人員反應。目前在等候室為旅客備有歐式早餐，整個上午都有餐點供應，請自由取用咖啡、茶、麵包及水果。新的航班時間決定後將馬上告知，現在請暫時放輕鬆，保持耐性，並祝各位有一個美好的早晨。

## 71.

答案：(C) 機場

中譯：這段廣播是在哪裡播送的？

(A) 火車車站　　　　　　　　　　(B) 旅行社的辦公室

(C) 機場　　　　　　　　　　　　(D) 咖啡店

題解：此題答案可由開頭的 Attention, Trans Air passengers. 來判斷，如果聽漏了，由 flights from Hong Kong have been delayed 等內容仍可得知廣播進行的場所。

## 72.

答案：(D) 暴風雨

中譯：香港的天氣如何？

(A) 有霧　　　　　　　　　　　　(B) 晴天

(C) 飄著小雪　　　　　　　　　　(D) 暴風雨

**題解**：可由第 2 句的 Due to unusually strong storms... 等判斷，本文出現的 storm 是名詞，選擇題使用形容詞 stormy。

## 73. 🎧 ········································································

**答案**：(A) 早上

**中譯**：這段廣播是在哪個時間播出？

    (A) 早上                 (B) 下午

    (C) 傍晚                 (D) 深夜

**題解**：答案可由後段內容中所說，準備 continental breakfast「歐式早餐」、可由 all morning「整個早上」取用得知，或從最後 have a good morning 中也可判斷。

---

### 閱讀測驗

---

### READING TEST

In the Reading test, you will read a variety of texts and answer several types o f reading comprehension questions. The entire Reading test will last 75 minutes. There are three parts, and directions are given for each part. You are encouraged to answer as many questions as possible within the time allowed.

You must mark your answer on the separate answer sheet. Do not write your answer in the test book.

# PART 5

**Directions** : A word or phrase is missing in each of the sentences below. Four answer choices are given below each sentence. Select the best answer to complete the sentence. Then mark the letter (A), (B), (C), or (D) on your answer sheet.

**101.** Register early if you would like to attend next Tuesday's _____ on project management.

(A) seminar      (B) reason      (C) policy      (D) scene

🌐 中譯

### 閱讀測驗

在閱讀測驗中,你會看到不同的文字類型,請回答不同的閱讀理解問題。完整的閱讀測驗長約 75 分鐘。共有 3 個部分,每一部分將有作答說明。你必須在有限時間內盡可能回答問題。

請在答案紙上畫記你的答案。請勿在試題本上書寫答案。

本部分包含 40 題，每一題有一個空格，請從每題的四個選項中，選出最適合的答案，使句子完整。

● 題解

## 101. 🎧

**答案：**(A) 研討會

**中譯：**希望出席下週二專案管理研討會的人，請儘早報名。

(A) 研討會　　　　　　　　(B) 理由

(C) 政策　　　　　　　　　(D) 場景

**題解：**要作為 if 後的述語動詞 attend「出席 ~」的受詞，最適當的就是 (A) seminar「研討會」。

## PART 6

**Directions** : Read the texts below. A word or phrase is missing in some of the sentences. For each empty space in the text, select the best answer to complete the text. Then mark the letter (A), (B), (C), or (D) on your answer sheet.

Questions 141-144 refer to the following letter.

Ms. Monica Eisenman

555 King Street

Auckland

New Zealand

Dear Ms. Eisenman:

    I am _____ to confirm our offer of part-time employment at Western

**141.**

(A) pleased                     (B) pleasing

(C) pleasant                (D) pleasure

Enterprise.

    In your role as research assistant, you will report to Dr. Emma Walton, who will keep you informed of your specific duties and projects. Because you will be working with confidential information, you will be expected to _____ the

**142.**

(A) follow                      (B) advise

(C) imagine                 (D) require

enclosed employee code-of-ethics agreement.

    As we discussed, you will be paid twice a month _____ the

**143.**

(A) accords                   (B) according

(C) according to            (D) accordance with

company's normal payroll schedule. As an hourly employee working fewer than twenty hours per week, you will not be _____ to receive paid

**144.**

(A) tolerable

(B) liberal

(C) eligible

(D) expressed

holidays, paid time off for illness or vacation, or other employee benefits. Your employment status will be reviewed in six months.

If you have any questions, please feel free to contact me. Otherwise, please sign and return one copy of this letter. You may keep the second copy for your files. We look forward to working with you.

Sincerely,

Christopher Webster

Human Resources

Enclosures

中譯

PART 6：（段落填空 / 12 題）

請閱讀以下短文，每篇短文有 4 個空格，每個空格有四個選項，請選出最適合的答案，使整篇文章完整，在答案紙上畫記 (A)、(B)、(C) 或 (D)。

# 141 ～ 144.

原文翻譯：

Monica Eisenman 小姐

國王街 555 號

奧克蘭

紐西蘭

親愛的 Eisenman 小姐：

很高興通知您，本公司將雇用您為 Western Enterprises 的兼職人員。身為 Emma Walton 博士的研究助理，所有事皆向她報告，她會告訴您具體的職務以及專案。由於您的工作內容有高度機密性，請遵守附件的公司員工道德規範同意書。

誠如之前我們的討論，每個月您將分領兩次支薪，根據本公司訂定的發薪日。由於您是一週工作時間少於二十小時的時薪員工，休假無薪水，也不適用病假與休假規定及其他福利，雇用契約每六個月更新一次。

若有任何問題，請儘管與我聯繫。若沒有其他特別的問題，請簽名並寄回一份給我，您可保留另一份存檔。我們期待與您一起工作。

Christopher Webster

人力資源部 謹上

有附件

# 141.

**答案**：(A) 樂意的

**題解**：pleased 是形容詞，be pleased to + 動詞 是標準書信所常用的尊敬語，有「樂意～」的意思。(B) 是形容詞，「令人舒適、愉快的」。(C) 是形容詞，將事物當作主語是「令人愉快的」，人當主語是「討人喜歡的」。(D) 是名詞，「高興、樂趣」。

# 142.

**答案**：(A) 遵守、依照

**題解**：選項全部是動詞，之後接下來的「附件的公司成員道德規範同意書」是受詞，適當的動詞由前後文來判斷，應為 follow「遵守（規定等）、依照～」。

# 143.

**答案**：(C) 依照、根據

**題解**：according to～是「依照～、根據～」，本文的 payroll schedule 為「薪資支付時間」。(A) accords 是「一致」的名詞複數形，以及「一致」動詞的第三人稱單數形，這個選項不符合文法。(B) according 並不能單獨使用，應用 according to。(D) 若是 in accordance with 是「依照～」的意思，但因為沒有 in 所以錯了。

# 144.

**答案**：(C) 有……資格的

**題解**：空格之後有不定詞，由文意來看，eligible 是最適當的，be eligible to～ 是「有～的資格」。(A) 是形容詞，「可忍受的」。(B) 是形容詞，「心胸寬大的」。(D) expressed 是動詞的 express「表達」的過去分詞

# PART 7

**Directions** : In this part you will read a selection of texts, such as magazine and newspaper articles, letters, and advertisements. Each text is followed by several questions. Select the best answer for each question and mark the letter (A), (B), (C), or (D) on your answer sheet.

Questions 153-155 refer to the following advertisement.

## Italian Food at its Finest…The Venezia

Under New Ownership

Open 7days, 11A.M.-11P.M.

| **Coupon** | **Coupon** | **Coupon** |
|---|---|---|
| **$2 off** | **50% Off** | **$2 off** |
| Any order over $10 with this coupon. Not valid with other offers. Offer good until June 16. | Buy 1 meal, get 2nd one 50% off with this coupon. Not valid with other offers. Offer good until June 16. | 1 liter of soda with delivery with this coupon. Not valid with other offers. Offer good until June 16. |

**153.** What is the purpose of this advertisement?

(A) To announce a change in business hours

(B) To advertise a business for sale

(C) To encourage diners to eat early

(D) To attract more customers

**154.** What will customers receive if they spend more than $10?

(A) A $2 discount on their bill

(B) 50% off their next purchase

(C) A liter of soda

(D) Free delivery service

**155.** What will happen on June 16?

(A) A new owner will take over the business.

(B) The coupons will expire.

(C) Prices will be further reduced.

(D) The business will close.

**PART 7：〔閱讀測驗 / 48 題〕**

本部分包括數篇不同題材的文章，例如雜誌、報紙文章、信件或廣告，每篇文章對應數道試題，每道試題有四個選項，請選出最適當的答案，在答案紙上畫記 (A)、(B)、(C) 或 (D)。

● 題解

# 153～155.

短文翻譯：

最棒的義大利料理……在威尼斯

全新開張

每日營業 營業時間上午 11 時～晚上 11 時

| 優待券<br>折扣 2 美元 | 優待券<br>折扣 50% | 優待券<br>免費 |
|---|---|---|
| 結帳超過 10 美元即可抵用，不可與其他優惠併用，至 6 月 16 日有效。 | 第一份餐點原價，第二份餐點可享半價，不可與其他優惠併用，至 6 月 16 日有效。 | 訂購外送餐點，贈送一公升汽水，不可與其他優惠併用，至 6 月 16 日有效。 |

# 153.

**答案：** (D) 招攬更多的客人

**中譯：** 這個廣告的目的為何？

(A) 通知營業時間變更　　　　　　(B) 告知店面出售

(C) 建議顧客提早用餐　　　　　　(D) 招攬更多的客人

**題解：** 可從 COUPON「優待券」或 off「折扣」、FREE「免費」這幾個字詞來判斷。

(A) business hours「營業時間」在第 3 行有寫到，但這並非廣告目的。

(B) sale 指的是「銷售」。

(C) diner「吃飯的客人」。

# 154.

**答案：** (A) 2 美元的折扣

**中譯：** 若買比 10 美元更多的話，客戶會有什麼優惠呢？

(A) 2 美元的折扣　　　　　　　　(B) 下一次消費可享五折

(C) 得到一公升的汽水　　　　　　(D) 免費外送服務

**題解：** More than $10「比 10 美元多」是指最左邊的 COUPON 的 Any order over $10「點餐超過 10 美元」。

(B) purchase 是「購買」，但這裡指的是購買的食物，這項優惠是針對點用第二份套餐的服務。

(C) A liter of soda 是右邊的 COUPON，是點餐外送的優惠。

(D) 免費外送是每張優待券上都沒有提到的。

# 155.

**答案：**(B) 優待券期限到期。

**中譯：**6 月 16 日將發生什麼事？

    (A) 新的老闆將接手這家店。       (B) 優待券期限到期。

    (C) 價格將更低。             (D) 店家結束營業。

**題解：**expire「截止日期」，全部 COUPON 的最下方的 good 是「有效的」，until June 16「到 6 月 16 日」，offer 是「提供」的意思，指此 COUPON。

(A) take over「接手～」，試題中第二行的 New Ownership「新老闆」，和 6 月 16 日並沒有寫在一起。(C) further「進一步」，reduce「降低」。

# 本書分類說明

多益測驗是以職場常用的溝通內容為範圍，《TOEIC 900（Ⅰ）》、《TOEIC 900（Ⅱ）》共選取 90 則在職場中常會運用到的句法，並且依照溝通的目的將這些句法歸納成 4 個類別，分別是書信與公文、人際溝通、事物說明、及商務運作。

## 一、書信與公文：

包括如何表達信件的主旨、內容重點、客套用語、個人期望、附件說明等各種用詞，不論是正式的文件，或一般的電子郵件往來，讀者都可以活用書中介紹的動詞及片語。

## 二、人際溝通：

包括如何表達個人情緒（如謝意、歉意、歡喜、榮幸），與人互動的經驗（如報告、演說、要求、鼓勵、獎賞、抱怨），這些字詞句法，將可套用到許多生活面向，並增進個人表達能力。

## 三、事物說明：

包括對於事物本身的描述、位置、價值、選擇、替代、比較；另外還有對於事物的提供、利用、處理、捐獻等。提升讀者對於事物說明的遣詞用字能力。

## 四、商務運作：

介紹商務運作的五大要素：目的、金錢、時間、原因、事物發展，不但提供完整具體的專業表達方式，還能讓讀者熟悉一般商務運作的架構。

# 本書體例說明

《TOEIC 900（Ⅰ）》、《TOEIC 900（Ⅱ）》共涵蓋 90 則國際職場常用句法，在解釋這些句法時，依據下述措詞為原則：

1. 所使用的詞語都是以「白話」方式表達，避免使用文法專用術語。

2. 以符號取代專門術語，讓讀者一目了然。

3. 每種句法的中文說明都清楚傳達該句法的溝通目的。


## 體例說明：

1.「出現機率」代表該句型在 TOEIC 測驗中的出現頻率，以 5 顆星等級表示。

2. S 代表主詞，V 代表動詞。例如：S ＋ inform ＋ 人 ＋ that ＋ S ＋ V（通知某人某事）。

3. 如果句法中有兩個結構，分別都有 S 與 V，會以 S₁ ＋ V₁ 和 S₂ ＋ V₂ 區分。

　例如：S₁ ＋ V₁, while ＋ S₂ ＋ V₂（當……時候，雖然）

4. 以 to V 代表不定詞。

　例如：allow/ encourage/ request ＋ 人 ＋ to V（允許 / 鼓勵 / 要求＋某人做某事）

5. V-ing 代表現在分詞。

　例如：S ＋ am/ is/ are/ was/ were ＋ worth ＋ 事物 / V-ing（值得……）

6. 用具體的中英文字詞表達句法功能。

　例如：事物 / it ＋ take/ cost ＋ 時間 / 金錢 / 事物（花費；消耗）

　本句法的主詞是「事物 / it」，受詞是「時間 / 金錢 / 事物」。

7. 利用 "／" 符號區分句子的結構，並且依據該結構做中文翻譯。

　例如：Enclosed/ is/ a copy of the form signed by Mr. Beeson.

　　　（隨函附上的 / 是 / 一份由 Beeson 先生簽署的表格）

# TOEIC 900

## 句型解說及練習

II

# Part A

## Texts
## 書信與公文

包括如何表達信件的主旨、內容重點、客套用語、個人期望、附件說明等各種用詞,不論是正式文件,或一般的電子郵件往來,讀者都可以活用書中介紹的動詞及片語。

# 句法 1
## 根據

## According to ＋ 資料、報導、人或機構 / 標準（根據……所說 / 按照）

### 🌐 例句

1. **According to** the news,/ there were an estimated 100 people/ trapped in the building/ at the time of the fire.

   （根據新聞報導 / 估計有一百人 / 被困在大樓裡 / 當火災發生時）

2. **According to** the Medical Association,/ Monday morning at approximately 10:00 a.m./ is the most common time for a heart attack.

   （根據醫療學會所言 / 週一上午大約十點 / 是心臟病最容易發作的時刻）

3. Mr. Frederickson asked his secretary/ to classify the documents/ **according to** the four business areas.

   （Frederickson 先生要求他的秘書 / 將資料分類 / 按照四個商業區域）

### 🌐 說明

According to ＋資料、報導、人或機構 / 標準（根據……所說 / 按照），在多益試題中通常有兩種意義：其一是根據某種客觀數據、事實或某人 / 機構，敘述某種看法或結論；其二是按照某個標準，進行某種行為。常出現在商務或科技情境。

### 🌐 常見用法

a）According to ＋ 資料,＋ S ＋ V（如例句第一、例句第二句）

According to 常放在句首，後面的 S＋V 敘述歸納出的看法或結論。

b）S＋V＋according to＋標準（如例句第三句）

## 多益擬真測驗

_____ **1. According to** a _____ conducted by _Technology Magazine_, the diffusion of broadband technology in society has skyrocketed in the past three years.

　　a）regulation　　　b）policy　　　c）survey　　　d）party

_____ **2. According to** a report, the effects of global warming will be felt _____ as hurricanes increase not only in frequency but also in intensity.

　　a）sinisterly　　b）significantly　　c）presumably　　d）profoundly

_____ **3. According to** EB Airport security _____ , passengers who refuse to submit to a full body X-ray scan will be prohibited from boarding an airplane.

　　a）regulations　　b）repairmen　　c）repetitions　　d）rehearsals

第 4-1 ～ 4-2 題，請聽簡短獨白，選擇適當的答案 🎧 06

_____ **4 - 1.** What do most of the mail thieves have in common?

　　a）They work at the post office.　　b）They have no fixed address.

　　c）They are drug users.　　d）They are surprised when mail is missing.

_____ **4 - 2.** What has the post office done to combat theft?

　　a）Brought in more postal inspectors.

　　b）Put locks on all mailboxes.

　　c）Increased the fine and jail time for offenders.

　　d）Introduced special services for customers.

# 句法 2

## 描述可能性

## whether + S + V（是否……）

### 🔵 例句

1. I wonder/ **whether** James has left the country/ as I haven't seen him for some time.

   （我在想 / James 是不是已經出國 / 因為我已經有段時間沒看到他了）

2. The hillside residents had to decide/ **whether** to evacuate their homes/ in the path of an approaching super typhoon.

   （山坡邊的居民必須決定 / 是否撤離家園 / 在即將來襲的超級颱風路徑上）

3. Recently,/ the availability of new, promising drugs/ has raised the dilemma of/ **whether** benefits outweigh the risks.

   （最近 / 使用有療效的新藥 / 引發爭議 / 是否其助益大於風險）

### 🔵 說明 ......

whether + S + V（是否……）用來表示對於某件事情不確定或提出疑問；whether 所引導的句子可當作一句話，作為主詞或受詞。

### 🔵 常見用法 ......

a ) S + V + whether + S + V（+ or not）（如例句第一句）

b ) S + V + whether + to V（+ or not）（如例句第二句）

c ) S + V + N + of + whether + S + V（+ or not）（如例句第三句）

## 多益擬真測驗

_____ **1.** _____ Mr. White will succeed in this business or not depends on his effort and luck.

a ) If          b ) What          c ) Whether          d ) Which

_____ **2.** _____, at least to residents of the small town who have only just recovered from last year's forest fire, is **whether** the dryness of the winter will last through to summer.

a ) Once major concerning          b ) One major concern

c ) Once concern majored          d ) One concerned major

_____ **3.** Australian athletes must make their own _____ about **whether** to go to the Commonwealth Games in New Delhi as the travel warning remains in place.

a ) investment     b ) decision     c ) precision     d ) derision

第 4-1 ～ 4-2 題，請聽簡短獨白，選擇適當的答案 🎧 **07**

_____ **4 - 1.** What happened in the south Puget Sound region?

a ) An anti-government demonstration  b ) Flooding

c ) A windstorm          d ) A store robbery

_____ **4 - 2.** What time of day did the problem begin?

a ) Early evening          b ) Early morning

c ) Midday          d ) Midnight

# 句法 3
## 聯絡、接觸

出現機率：★★★★★

## contact/ reach/ connect ＋ 人 / 機構（聯繫；接觸 / 接通）

### 🔵 例句

1. Please **contact** the store/ from which you bought your Orlando product/ for a refund, exchange, or repair.

（請聯繫該商店 / 您購買奧蘭多產品的地方 / 以便退款、換貨或維修）

2. If there are any changes,/ you can **reach** me/ in Vancouver at 360-555-4363.

（如有任何變動 / 您可以聯繫我 / 使用溫哥華 360-555-4363 的電話）

3. If you are outside of the office,/ just dial the main company number/ and let the operator **connect** you/ to the right extension number.

（如果你人在辦公室外 / 只要撥打公司代表號 / 讓總機幫你轉接 / 到正確的分機號碼）

### 🔵 說明

contact/ reach/ connect ＋ 人 / 機構（聯繫；接觸 / 接通），在職場中用來表示與人或與商家之間的聯繫、互動；常出現在商業書信或電話聯絡的對話情境。

### 🔵 常見用法

a）contact ＋ 人 / 機構（如例句第一句）

b）reach ＋ 人 / 機構（如例句第二句）

c）connect ＋ 人 / 機構（＋ to 號碼 / 聯絡對象）（如例句第三句）

connect 在此句法專指接通電話或網路。

## 多益擬真測驗

_____ **1.** Callers who could not **reach** the intended recipient owing to _____ signals will be diverted to the voice mail system.

a ) busy      b ) available      c ) accessible      d ) ready

_____ **2.** Please do not _____ to **contact** the personnel office if you have questions about the job description procedures.

a ) hurry      b ) hesitate      c ) head      d ) hustle

_____ **3.** With major winter storms making the news and attracting visitors to the Forest Park, please equip yourself with satellite _____ , which **connect** you to 911 at the touch of a finger in case of emergency.

a ) dishes      b ) centers      c ) television      d ) phones

第 4-1 ～ 4-2 題，請聽簡短獨白，選擇適當的答案 🎧 08

_____ **4 - 1.** What can a person do on the telephone when hearing this message?

a ) Receive counseling.      b ) Speak to their family.

c ) Cancel an appointment.      d ) Purchase healing books.

_____ **4 - 2.** When is this office open?

a ) Monday through Saturday      b ) Twenty-four hours a day

c ) 10:00 a.m. to 9:00 p.m.      d ) Seven days a week

# 句法 4

## 提醒

出現機率：★★☆☆☆

## 人 / 機構 / 事物＋ remind ＋ 人 ＋ that/ to-V/ of（提醒 / 想起）

### 📀 例句

1. We would like to **remind** you/ that you are eligible/ to give blood again/ four weeks after your last donation.

   （我們想要提醒您 / 您有資格 / 再次捐血 / 在上次捐血四週之後）

2. The Elm Valley Police Department/ has come up with an ingenious way/ to **remind** drivers/ to keep their cars within local speed limits.

   （榆樹谷警察局 / 想到一個妙招 / 提醒駕駛人 / 將車子保持在當地速限範圍內）

3. The fresh new scent of Nadia Combo perfume/ **reminds** one **of** /springtime and lemons.

   （Nadia Combo 香水的清新氣味 / 讓人憶及 / 春日時光和檸檬芬芳）

### 📀 說明

remind ＋ 人 ＋ that/ to-V/ of（提醒 / 想起），用來表示提醒某人去做某件事情，或是讓某人想起之前經歷過的事物。

### 📀 常見用法

a）人 / 機構 ＋ remind ＋ 人 ＋ that ＋ S ＋ V（如例句第一句）

b）人 / 機構 ＋ remind ＋ 人 ＋ to-V（如例句第二句）

　　a 與 b 的句法都是指提醒某人做某事。

c）人／事物1＋ remind ＋人＋ of ＋人／事物2（如例句第三句）

c 句法是指人／事物1讓某人想起記憶中的人／事物2。

## 多益擬真測驗

_____ **1.** Since summer is right-around-the-corner, we would like to _____ you how to run your room air conditioner.

    a）remember      b）remind      c）retrieve      d）remain

_____ **2.** We would like to **remind** you that your account of 1,998 Euros is _____ ; if there is a particular reason for failing to remit the payment, please call us.

    a）overripe      b）immature      c）past due      d）well-balanced

_____ **3.** WorkOrganizer is a powerful time management software program which will help you track your tasks effectively and **remind** you **of** _____.

    a）deadends      b）deadlocks      c）deadlines      d）deadbolts

第 4-1 ～ 4-2 題，請聽簡短獨白，選擇適當的答案 🎧 **09**

_____ **4 - 1.** Where does this announcement take place?

    a）At a swimming pool      b）In a hotel

    c）At a public beach      d）By a harbor

_____ **4 - 2.** When does this announcement take place?

    a）At sunset      b）At lunchtime

    c）In the morning      d）Late at night

# 句法 5

## 確信－1

## 人／機構 ＋ am/ is/ was/ are/ were ＋ certain/ sure/ positive ＋ of/ that（確定）

### 🔵 例句

1. We could be fairly **certain** about/ the existence of an outbreak/ as more H1N1 cases were reported in this area.

   （我們可以非常確定／疫情爆發／當此地區被通報更多 H1N1 病例）

2. Some financial analysts/ are **sure**/ that the stock price will go up/ after the announcement of a merger/ between the two business entities.

   （一些財務分析師／確定／股價會走高／在發佈合併之後／在兩家企業實體之間）

3. The government is absolutely **positive**/ that infrastructure improvement/ should be the top priority/ in this country.

   （政府非常確定／基礎建設的改善／應該是當務之急／在這個國家）

### 🔵 說明

人／機構 ＋ am/ is/ was/ are/ were ＋ certain/ sure/ positive ＋ of/ that（確定），常用於表達對某件事情的確定態度。

### 🔵 常見用法

a) 人／機構 ＋ am/ is/ was/ are/ were ＋ certain/ sure/ positive ＋ about/ of ＋ 事物（如例句第一句）

b）人／機構 ＋ am/ is/ was/ are/ were ＋ certain/ sure/ positive ＋ that ＋ S ＋ V（如例句第二及例句第三句）

## 多益擬真測驗

_____ **1.** You may use a checklist before your _____ to be sure that you are properly prepared and confident of getting the job.

    a）inception      b）inspection      c）interrogation      d）interview

_____ **2.** We are quite **certain** that population growth and fossil fuel _____ are closely related to golbal warming.

    a）exception      b）consumption      c）consumer      d）extinction

_____ **3.** The analysts are **positive** that the new product, which is in a lower price range, will sell _____ than its predecessor.

    a）better      b）worse      c）most      d）least

第 4-1 ～ 4-2 題，請聽簡短獨白，選擇適當的答案 🎧**10**

_____ **4 - 1.** Where does this announcement take place?

    a）At a camp               b）At a hospital

    c）At a health club        d）At a school

_____ **4 - 2.** What must be signed?

    a）A sales contract        b）A sign-in sheet

    c）A health form           d）A file

# 句法 6
## 確信 – 2

出現機率：★★☆☆☆

## 人／機構／措施 ＋ ensure ＋ 情況／ that ＋ S ＋ V（確保……）

### 🌐 例句

1. Maintaining a regular regime/ of carpet cleaning/ can **ensure**/ longevity of the carpet/ and good indoor air quality.

（保持定期制度／清潔地毯／可確保／地毯的壽命／及良好室內空氣品質）

2. A food service manager/ should **ensure**/ that the food establishment is running smoothly/ to meet customer satisfaction goals.

（餐飲經理／應確保／餐飲產製運作順暢／達到顧客滿意目標）

3. The company provides computer training/ to **ensure**/ that every employee has the latest computer knowledge and skills.

（公司提供電腦訓練／以確保／每位員工具備最新的電腦知識及技能）

### 🌐 說明

人／機構／措施 ＋ ensure ＋ 情況／ that ＋ S ＋ V（確保……），用來表達確保某件事情會運作正常或順利。

### 🌐 常見用法

a) 人／機構／措施 ＋ ensure ＋ 情況（如例句第一句）

b) 人／機構／措施 ＋ ensure ＋ that ＋ S ＋ V（如例句第二句）

c) S ＋ V ＋ to ensure ＋情況／ that ＋ S ＋ V（如例句第三句）

由於「確保某事順利運作」屬於一種「目標性的陳述」，因此 to ensure 這類表示目的性的句法是最普遍的；句中的 S + V 是表示要採取的作法或措施。

## 多益擬真測驗

_____ **1.** Please mail your payment at least five business days before the due date to _____ that it arrives on time.

    a ) include      b ) clarify      c ) ensure      d ) defend

_____ **2.** Hairnets are required to **ensure** that no foreign _____ get into the products on the assembly line.

    a ) visitors      b ) policies      c ) objects      d ) objectives

_____ **3.** Our PR team will place your contributed copy in key publications across Europe to **ensure** maximum _____ for your new product in this area.

    a ) exposition      b ) exposure      c ) exit      d ) exhilaration

第 4-1 ～ 4-2 題，請聽簡短獨白，選擇適當的答案 🎧 **11**

_____ **4 - 1.** How can this company best be described?

    a ) A travel company      b ) A moving company

    c ) A company in Alaska      d ) A rental truck company

_____ **4 - 2.** Where does this company provide services?

    a ) Only the Western United States      b ) North America and Europe

    c ) Worldwide      d ) Only North America

# 句法 7
## 表示應做之事

出現機率：★★★★☆

## 人／事物 ＋ be supposed to ＋ V（應該）

### 🔵 例句

1. A wedding reception/ **is supposed to** be fun and enjoyable,/ so it is important to/ carefully select your venue, food, and decorations.

（結婚宴會／應該是有趣而歡樂的／因此重要的是／慎選場地、餐點和裝潢）

2. The airplane **was supposed to**/ take off at 3 o' clock,/ but the airline had to cancel the flight/ because of a blizzard.

（飛機應該／在三點起飛／但是航空公司必須取消航班／因為一場大風雪）

3. Both parties/ **are not supposed to**/ reveal the content of the contract/ to a third party/ until the contract is signed.

（雙方／不應／透露合約內容／給第三者／直到合約簽訂）

### 🔵 說明

人／事物 ＋ be supposed to ＋ V（應該），通常有三種意思表示：

a）表示事情應該是如此的，如例句第一句。

b）表示應該如此，但實際狀況並非如此，如例句第二句。

c）be ＋ not supposed to，表示事情不應如此處理，如例句第三句。

## 🌐 常見用法

　　a）人／事物＋be supposed to＋V（如例句第一、例句第二句）。

　　b）人／事物＋be＋not supposed to＋V（如例句第三句）。

### 多益擬真測驗

_____ **1.** Employees **are supposed to** follow the _____ code and wear formal attire when attending sales conferences on behalf of our company.

　　a）pin 　　　　　b）moral 　　　　c）penal 　　　　d）dress

_____ **2.** Mr. Sato **was supposed to** attend the convention, but in the end, Ms. Chen _____ him.

　　a）changed 　　　b）replaced 　　　c）instead of 　　　d）relocated

_____ **3.** Vehicle users **are not supposed to** park their cars on a yellow curb and will pay a _____ for this illegal behavior.

　　a）fine 　　　　　b）attention 　　　c）fee 　　　　　d）tax

第 4-1 ～ 4-2 題，請聽簡短獨白，選擇適當的答案 🎧 12

_____ **4 - 1.** What are Frank and Stella going to do this weekend?

　　a）Go to a barbecue party 　　　　b）Go camping

　　c）Go to a concert 　　　　　　　　d）Go to a beach party

_____ **4 - 2.** How is Frank supposed to receive this message from Stella?

　　a）From an answering machine 　　　b）By a P.A. announcement

　　c）From a friend 　　　　　　　　　d）In person

# 句法 8
## 說明地點

## 建築 / 設備 / 場所 ＋ be located/ situated ＋ in ＋ 位置（位於）

### 🌐 例句

1. The subsidiaries of Lines Company/ **are** all **located** in big cities/ such as New York, London, and Tokyo.

（Lines 公司各分公司 / 都位於大城市 / 像是紐約、倫敦、東京）

2. Klein Garden House **is** ideally **situated**/ for accessing all the attractions/ of the North West of England.

（Klein 花園賓館理想地座落在 / 能方便至各景點 / 英格蘭西北地區）

3. Our company works with 400 hospitals/ **located** throughout the U.S.,/ with new hospitals being added daily.

（我們公司與四百家醫院有往來 / 位於全美各地 / 新的合作對象正與日俱增）

### 🌐 說明

建築 / 設備 / 場所 ＋ be located/ situated ＋ in ＋ 位置（位於），表示某個場所的地理位置，常出現在多益測驗談論公司或辦公室地點的情境。

### 🌐 常見用法

a ) 建築 / 設備 / 場所 ＋ be located/ situated ＋ in ＋ 位置（如例句第一句）

b ) 建築 / 設備 / 場所 ＋ be located/ situated ＋ for ＋ 功能 / 目的（如例句第二句）

located/ situated 後面可接 in, at, on, near, throughout 表示地理位置，接 for 表示功能或目的。

c ) 建築／設備／場所 ＋ located/ situated（如例句第三句）

located/ situated 放在建築物／場所之後，來修飾該地點或場所。

## 多益擬真測驗

_____ **1.** For your safety, there **are** four _____ **located** throughout this aircraft.

    a ) passengers     b ) crew members     c ) emergency exits    d ) dining cars

_____ **2.** White Cliffs Hotel **is located** atop a 350 foot cliff, _____ the beautiful Mediterranean Sea.

    a ) overbooking     b ) overcrowding     c ) overlooking     d ) overwhelming

_____ **3.** Episcopal Convention Centre **is situated** in Liverpool City centre, and with easy _____ to all transport routes; you can't find a more ideal event venue.

    a ) entry     b ) access     c ) exit     d ) accretion

第 4-1 ～ 4-2 題，請聽簡短獨白，選擇適當的答案 🎧 13

_____ **4 - 1.** Who is this advertisement for?

    a ) Aspiring nurses        b ) Experienced American nurses

    c ) Nurses who want to work overseas    d ) Nurses who live in cold places

_____ **4 - 2.** Where will nurses who qualify be placed?

    a ) In Florida, California or Hawaii     b ) Somewhere overseas

    c ) In the state the nurse chooses      d ) Wherever nurses are most needed

# 句法 9

## 報告

## 人／機構＋report＋事件（報告；舉發；描述）

### ● 例句

1. Clare County Rescue Service/ **reported**/ a decrease in the number of road traffic incidents/ in the first eight months of 2009.

（Clare 郡救援服務／報告／道路交通事故的數量減少／在 2009 年前八個月）

2. Mr. Sykes/ **reports**/ that the driver refused to take the goods back,/ contrary to your company's stated policy.

（Sykes 先生／舉發／司機拒絕將貨物取回／有違你們公司既定的政策）

3. No deaths or injuries/ were **reported**/ in the fire accident last night.

（沒有死傷／據報導／在昨晚的火災事故中）

### ● 說明

report（報告；描述），常用來表示對一般大眾或是特定對象報告或描述某個事件，此類句法常出現在多益聽力測驗中。

### ● 常見用法

a）人／機構＋report＋事件（如例句第一句）

b）人／機構＋report＋that＋S＋V（如例句第二句）

c）事件＋be reported＋時間或地點的字詞（如例句第三句）

62

## 多益擬真測驗

_____ **1.** Most research on this on-the-job training program **reports** positive effects; there is a significant _____ in performance for employees who participated for 30 days or more.

　a ) implication　　b ) image　　　　c ) improvement　　d ) deterioration

_____ **2.** Residents in Kalihi _____ illegal dumping in their neighborhood, complaining that it was getting worse and posed a potential health risk.

　a ) answered　　b ) reported　　　c ) told　　　　　d ) regarded

_____ **3.** A clerk at a convenience store on East Wellington Street **reported** that an acquaintance _____ him and said he would rob the store that night.

　a ) consoled　　b ) advised　　　c ) recommended　　d ) threatened

第 4-1 ～ 4-2 題，請聽簡短獨白，選擇適當的答案 🎧 14

_____ **4 - 1.** How much damage did the earthquake cause?

　a ) A great deal　　　　　　　b ) A small amount

　c ) Some people were injured.　　d ) A few buildings collapsed.

_____ **4 - 2.** When did the earthquake occur?

　a ) Early in the morning　　　　b ) During the afternoon commute

　c ) During the morning commute　　d ) In the middle of the day

# 句法 10

## 授予獎勵

## 人／機構＋ award ＋人／機構＋事物（授予；給予）

### 例句

1. The city government / **awarded** him/ a license/ to build 40,000 low-cost apartment units/ in the suburban area.

   （市政府／授予他／執照／興建四萬間低成本公寓／在郊區）

2. The official/ **awarded**/ the project/ to the company/ with the fifth-lowest bid/ and the third-highest overall ranking/ among seven competitors.

   （官員／授予／專案／給一間公司／以第五低的投標價／總排名第三高／在七個競爭者中）

3. Our firm/ has recently been **awarded**/ the contract/ for the design of a large public swimming facility/ in Malaysia.

   （我們公司／最近獲得／合約／大型公共游泳設施的設計／在馬來西亞）

### 說明

award ＋人／機構＋事物（授予），代表在公開場合正式授予某「人／機構」某種「事物」，所謂「事物」係指某種獎勵、權利、或合約的取得；通常出現在多益的人事或商業企劃情境。

### 常見用法

a）人／機構＋ award ＋人／機構＋事物（如例句第一句）

b）人／機構 ＋ award ＋ 事物 ＋ to ＋ 人／機構（如例句第二句）

c）人／機構 ＋ be awarded ＋ 事物（如例句第三句）

若將事物當作主詞句法如右：事物 ＋ be awarded to ＋ 人／機構

## 多益擬真測驗

_____ **1.** The researcher was **awarded** £20,000 to analyze the _____ of constructing a dam on the River Bourne.

a）flexibility　　　b）mobility　　　c）feasibility　　　d）accordance

_____ **2.** The City Government **awarded** the street-cleaning _____ to a sanitation company as more cities put services out to bid to take advantage of competitive pricing.

a）trophy　　　b）contract　　　c）prize　　　d）medal

_____ **3.** London was awarded the right to _____ the 2012 Olympic Games, narrowly defeating European rival Paris in the final round of voting.

a）host　　　b）cost　　　c）guest　　　d）hose

第 4-1 ～ 4-2 題，請聽簡短獨白，選擇適當的答案 🎧 15

_____ **4 - 1.** What is the purpose of the event?

a）To celebrate a new merger　　　b）To honor workers

c）To plan next year's strategies　　　d）To announce profits

_____ **4 - 2.** How can you get tickets to the banquet?

a）Go to the hotel.　　　b）Call the president.

c）Contact the board of directors.　　　d）Telephone the personnel office.

# Part B

# Persons
# 人際溝通

包括如何表達個人情緒（如謝意、歡意、歡喜、榮幸），與人互動的經驗（如報告、演說、要求、鼓勵、獎賞、抱怨），這些字詞句法，將可套用到許多生活面向，並增進個人表達能力。

## 人 / 機構 ＋ communicate/ negotiate ＋ with ＋人 / 機構（溝通 / 協商）

### 例句

1. If you can **communicate with** your employees/ with an approachable attitude,/ you will open the door/ for a free exchange of ideas.

   （如果你能與你的員工溝通 / 以平易近人的態度 / 你將開啟一扇門 / 自由地交換意見）

2. If you have a good credit record,/ you are in a favorable position/ to **negotiate** a lower interest rate/ **with** your bank.

   （如果你有良好的信用記錄 / 你居於有利的位置 / 協商更低的利率 / 與你的銀行）

### 說明

communicate/ negotiate ＋ with ＋人 / 機構（溝通 / 協商），最常用於會議的情境中。communicate 主要是將意見或概念傳達給對方；negotiate 則是為某種利害關係而進行談判或協商。

### 常見用法

a）人 / 機構 ＋ communicate/ negotiate ＋ with ＋人 / 機構（如例句第一句）

b）人 / 機構 ＋ negotiate ＋ 事物 ＋ with ＋人 / 機構（如例句第二句）

## 多益擬真測驗

_____ **1.** The NIL Board of Directors finally agreed to **negotiate with** the unions for better _____ for laid-off employees.

a ) penalties      b ) regulations      c ) merits      d ) benefits

_____ **2.** Setting carbon dioxide reduction _____ helps **communicate with** residents and allows them to achieve the desired reductions in time.

a ) targets      b ) tactics      c ) condition      d ) scenario

_____ **3.** If you cannot **negotiate** a lower rent **with** your _____ , it is still worth asking him if he can delay your payment.

a ) tenant      b ) landmark      c ) landlord      d ) distributor

第 4-1 ～ 4-2 題，請聽簡短獨白，選擇適當的答案 🎧 **16**

_____ **4 - 1.** What medium does Healthmaster use?

a ) The Internet      b ) A technical manual

c ) New computer hardware      d ) Phone messages

_____ **4 - 2.** What is this software designed to do?

a ) Provide medical training.

b ) Manage medical information.

c ) Announce important discoveries.

d ) Perform medical operations.

# 句法 2
## 表達想法

## it/ 事物 + occur to/ happen to（想到……/ 發生……）

### 例句

1. Some financial advisors/ like to use terminology,/ but it never **occurred to** them/ that their clients may not be comfortable/ with their choice of words.

   （有些財務顧問 / 喜歡使用術語 / 但是他們從未想到 / 他們的客戶可能感到不自在 / 對他們的用詞）

2. If sudden acceleration **happens to** your car,/ please try to step on the brake pedal/ with both feet/ using steady pressure/ and shift the transmission into neutral.

   （如果你的車子發生爆衝 / 請試著踩住剎車踏板 / 用雙腳 / 以平穩的壓力 / 並將變速器轉換到空檔）

### 說明

it/ 事物 + occur to/ happen to（想到……/ 發生……），occur to 說明心中想到某件事情；happen to 是表示事情的發生。

### 常見用法

a）it + occur to + 人 + that + S + V（如例句第一句）

it 指的是後面 that + S + V 所敘述的內容。occur to 前面也常以「事物」做主詞，例如 A good idea occurred to me.（我想到一個好主意。）

b ) 事物 ＋ happen to ＋ 人／事物（如例句第二句）

## 多益擬真測驗

_____ **1.** On my way to the conference venue, it **occurred to** me that I had forgotten to bring my meeting _____.

    a ) recipes      b ) documents      c ) dosage      d ) dockage

_____ **2.** Under these circumstances, there is no _____ what will **happen to** our company in the future.

    a ) procuring      b ) presenting      c ) predicting      d ) proposing

_____ **3.** It never _____ to us that this project could bring about such a dramatic lift in second-quarter profit.

    a ) happened      b ) occurred      c ) hatched      d ) occulted

第 4-1 ～ 4-2 題，請聽簡短獨白，選擇適當的答案 🎧 **17**

_____ **4 - 1.** Where did Derek Heinz create his work?

    a ) In the United States      b ) In Germany

    c ) In Europe      d ) In France

_____ **4 - 2.** What has happened to Martin's work in recent years?

    a ) It is undergoing a revival.

    b ) It is being performed less frequently.

    c ) It has been confused with other works.

    d ) It has been updated by modern artists.

# 句法 3
## 表達榮幸之意

出現機率：★★☆☆☆

## It ＋ is/ was/ would be ＋ a pleasure/ pity/ shame ＋ to V/ that 子句（樂事 / 憾事）

### 🔵 例句

1. **It would be a pleasure**/ for us/ to install new equipment for you/ at no charge.

（很高興 / 對我們來說 / 為你安裝新設備 / 免費）

2. **It was a pity**/ that we had to leave the conference early.

（很遺憾 / 我們必須提早離開會場）

3. I always enjoyed a meal at Alberto's;/ **it's a shame**/ that the restaurant had to close.

（我一直享受在 Alberto's 餐廳用餐的感覺 / 很遺憾 / 這家餐廳必須停止營業）

### 🔵 說明

a pleasure/ pity/ shame（樂事 / 憾事），用來表達對於一件事情的個人看法。pleasure 表示對某事感到快樂或榮幸；pity 及 shame 則表達遺憾的感覺。

### 🔵 常見用法

a）It ＋ is/ was/ would be ＋ a pleasure/ pity/ shame ＋ to V（如例句第一句）；it 指的 是 to V 所說的內容，pleasure/ pity/ shame 後面可以接 for sb. 表示對某人而言。

b）It ＋ is/ was/ would be ＋ a pleasure/ pity/ shame ＋ that ＋ S ＋ V（如例句第二、第 三句）；it 指的是 that 後面所說的內容。

## 多益擬真測驗

_____ **1. It is a pleasure** to _____ the contributions of our staff and many supporters, all of whom help to make Edinboro a place where great things truly do happen.

    a ) introduce      b ) acknowledge      c ) accentuate      d ) accede

_____ **2. It is a** _____ that he did not live to see the publication of his life's work.

    a ) pleasure      b ) priority      c ) party      d ) pity

_____ **3. It is a shame** that an institution founded on honor would resort to _____ in order to protect their reputation at the cost of the public interest.

    a ) decision      b ) deception      c ) derision      d ) deduction

第 4-1 ～ 4-3 題，請聽簡短獨白，選擇適當的答案 🎧 **18**

_____ **4 - 1.** Who is speaking?

    a ) St. Mary                 b ) Helen Park

    c ) The former president of the hospital      d ) The founder of the Sisters of the Poor

_____ **4 - 2.** How long has this hospital been established?

    a ) 96 years      b ) 75 years      c ) 20 years      d ) 10 years

_____ **4 - 3.** What is the origin of all worthwhile accomplishments?

    a ) Self-sacrificing groups or individuals      b ) Suffering peoples

    c ) Venerable Mother Helen Park      d ) The ideal of humanity

# 句法 4
## 表達歉意

出現機率：★★★★☆

## 人 / 機構＋apologize＋to 人＋for 事物（因某事對某人感到抱歉）

### 例句

1. We would like to **apologize for** the great inconvenience/ that this error may have caused you.

   （我們對於極大的不便道歉 / 這個錯誤所造成的）

2. Claudia said she despaired over her company/ because they didn't **apologize to** consumers/ after the misbranding scandal.

   （Claudia 說她對她的公司很失望 / 因為他們沒有向消費者致歉 / 在不實標示的醜聞之後）

3. TransAir **apologized to** stranded passengers/ **for** the unexpected delay/ caused by volcanic eruption.

   （TransAir 航空公司向滯留的旅客道歉 / 因為意外的延誤 / 由火山爆發造成的）

### 說明

apologize＋to 人＋for 事物（因某事對某人感到抱歉），在職場中表達歉意的正式用語。

### 常見用法

a) apologize＋for 事物（直接說明感到抱歉的事情，如例句第一句）

b) apologize＋to 人（表達對某人感到抱歉，如例句第二句）

c) apologize＋to 人＋for 事物（因為某事對某人感到抱歉，如例句第三句）

## 多益擬真測驗

_____ **1.** We _____ **for** the server outage that occurred during the restoration of a redundant disk system from a degraded state.

    a ) express      b ) apologize      c ) appreciate      d ) analyze

_____ **2.** We **apologize for** the fact that you did not sleep well in our motel last week due to _____ .

    a ) considerate service          b ) competitive prices

    c ) road construction noise      d ) money back guarantee

_____ **3.** In a statement, Joseph Donelly, the street artist, **apologized to** the citizens **for** posting his art in _____ spaces.

    a ) unauthorized      b ) legalized      c ) unitary      d ) unimportant

第 4-1 ～ 4-2 題，請聽簡短獨白，選擇適當的答案 🎧 19

_____ **4 - 1.** What is D.B. Mathews?

    a ) A grocery store          b ) A wholesaler

    c ) A credit card company      d ) A clothing store

_____ **4 - 2.** When will D.B. Mathews be open tomorrow?

    a ) It will be closed.

    b ) At the regular time

    c ) From 9:00 a.m. to 5:00 p.m.

    d ) Only in the morning

# 句法 5

## 表達抱怨

出現機率：★★☆☆☆

人 / 機構 ＋ file ＋ a complaint/ lawsuit/ claim ＋ against 人或機構 / for 理由（對……提出抱怨 / 訴訟 / 要求）

### 例句

1. Marco Island residents/ **filed a complaint** today/ against a nearby factory/ for violations of the noise control regulations.

   （Marco 島居民 / 今天提出抗議 / 針對附近一家工廠 / 因違反噪音管制法）

2. Bondex Corporation decided to/ **file a \$700 million lawsuit**/ against Sunaga Incorporated/ for patent infringement.

   （Bondex 公司決定 / 提出七億美元訴訟 / 針對 Sunaga 公司 / 因為專利侵權）

3. Consumers/ who purchase an item but later find the identical product at a cheaper price/ can **file a claim**/ with any of our branches/ for a refund of the difference.

   （消費者 / 購貨後發現同一商品有更便宜的價格 / 可以提出要求 / 跟我們任何一家分店 / 退還差價）

### 說明

file ＋ a complaint/ lawsuit/ claim ＋ against 人或機構 / for 理由（對……提出），是正式表達對某人或某機構提出抗議、訴訟或要求。常出現在多益測驗的顧客抱怨或申訴及商品購買情境。

## 常見用法

file ＋ a complaint/ lawsuit/ claim ＋ against/ with 人或機構 / for 理由

against 多用於抗議的對象之前；with 則用於可與之協商或幫助解決問題的對象之前。

## 多益擬真測驗

_____ **1.** Some members who had left this fitness center **filed a complaint** against it for continuing to send bills after membership had been _____.

a ) renovated      b ) retrieved      c ) cancelled      d ) conciliated

_____ **2.** CleanGround **filed a lawsuit** against FDC, alleging that the company _____ combined its garbage collection services with street-sweeping contracts.

a ) illegally      b ) legitimately      c ) leniently      d ) lectionary

_____ **3. File a complaint** against your _____ if you are harassed or fired for standing up for your rights as a worker to refuse an unsafe job.

a ) employee      b ) coworker      c ) emplacement      d ) employer

第 4-1 ～ 4-2 題，請聽簡短獨白，選擇適當的答案 🎧 20

_____ **4 - 1.** What has angered the union for Bering Aviation?

a ) The decision of the corporate executives      b ) The stockholders board

c ) The rumor of the company's move      d ) Economic pressures

_____ **4 - 2.** Why is Bering Aviation an exception?

a ) It has shut down its plants.    b ) It has come under fire with serious complaints.

c ) It is still an aeronautical manufacturer.    d ) It is still in the United States.

# 句法 6
## 選擇 – 1

## rather than（而不是……）

### 🔵 例句

1. Craig decided to turn down/ **rather than**/ accept the job offer.

   （Craig 決定拒絕 / 而非 / 接受該工作機會）

2. **Rather than**/ using formal business language,/ use conversational writing/ which will be more easily understood.

   （而不是 / 運用正式商業語言 / 運用口語書寫方式 / 較易被瞭解的）

### 🔵 說明

rather than（而不是……），在職場中通常用來表達兩個選項中，未被列入考慮的一方。如例句第一句選擇拒絕工作提議。

### 🔵 常見用法

a）選項一 ＋ rather than ＋ 選項二（如例句第一句）

   rather than 兩邊的選項是對等關係，使用相同詞性，如第一句兩邊都是動詞。

b）Rather than ＋ V/ V-ing, S ＋ V（如例句第二句，該句主詞為 you，此處省略）。

## 多益擬真測驗

_____ **1.** The report indicates that the AMbrook Fund is acting properly by delivering policy advice _____ **rather than** announcing it to the public.

a ) previously      b ) privately      c ) productively      d ) prestigiously

_____ **2.** _____ buying habits are usually influenced by word of mouth **rather than** book reviews.

a ) Readers'      b ) Authors'      c ) Performers'      d ) Publishers'

_____ **3. Rather than** attempting to avoid faults, we should realize that faults are unavoidable and instead focus on fault _____.

a ) relief      b ) tolerance      c ) exemption      d ) exuberance

第 4 題，請聽問題，選擇適當的回答

_____ **4.** Mark your answer on your answer sheet. 🎧 21

第 5 題，請聽簡短對話，選擇適當的答案

_____ **5.** Why did the man refuse the woman's offer? 🎧 22

a ) He would rather meet her somewhere else.

b ) She didn't offer properly.

c ) He is very religious.

d ) He is vegetarian.

# 句法 7
## 選擇 – 2

出現機率：★★★☆☆

## would rather/ would prefer to ＋ V（寧願做某事）

### 🔵 例句

1. Some people **would rather** live in a small town/ than in the city/ because the former is less polluted by traffic and noise.

   （有些人寧可住在小鎮／而非城市／因為前者較不會受到交通和噪音的汙染）

2. Jenny **would prefer to** come in sometime next week/ when her regular stylist is feeling better.

   （Jenny 寧願下週找時間再來／等她習慣的設計師身體好點時）

3. With the majority of the population/ **preferring** online shopping/ **to** store shopping,/ the percentage of online shoppers/ has passed the 50% mark.

   （隨著大多數人口／喜歡線上購物／勝過商店購物／線上購物者的比例／已超過一半）

### 🔵 說明

would rather/ would prefer to ＋ V（寧願做某事），都是表示在有選擇的情形下，寧可採取其中之一的選項。

### 🔵 常見用法

a）人／機構 ＋ would rather ＋ V（＋ than ＋不採取的選項）（如例句第一句，此句法的 than 後面省略了動詞 live。

b）人／機構＋(would) prefer to ＋V（如例句第二句）

c）人／機構＋prefer＋採取的選項（＋to ＋不採取的選項）（如例句第三句）

prefer 與 to 可以拆開來使用，分別接續兩種選項，喜歡 (prefer) 之後選項，而不喜歡 (to) 之後的選項。

## 多益擬真測驗

_____ **1.** Many companies **would rather** go with labor _____ than hire temporary or project-based employees.

a）hunting      b）accounting      c）outsourcing      d）resourcing

_____ **2.** One survey found that most U.S. parents **would rather** stay home and raise their children than work, if money were not an _____ .

a）interest      b）intervention      c）issue      d）assurance

_____ **3.** Sixty-eight percent of women **would prefer to** choose a pharmacy based on _____ and location, compared to only 48% of men, according to a study.

a）convenience      b）convention      c）circumvention      d）ventilation

第 4 題，請聽問題，選擇適當的回答 🎧 **23**

_____ **4.** Mark your answer on your answer sheet.

第 5 題，請聽簡短對話，選擇適當的答案 🎧 **24**

_____ **5.** Why doesn't the man drive to work?

a）Because cars pollute the air.      b）He prefers riding a motorcycle.

c）He prefers to exercise.      d）His friends told him not to.

# 句法 8

## 接受；認可

出現機率：★★★★★

## 人／機構＋accept/ approve＋人／事物（接受／認可）

### 🌐 例句

1. The CEO of Doe International/ **accepted**/ the resignation of the sales manager/ during their regular monthly meeting this morning.

（Doe 國際企業的執行長／接受／業務經理的辭職／在今天上午的例行月會中）

2. McLean County officials/ have **approved** a proposal/ to implement an in-house testing program/ on water quality in local streams.

（McLean 郡官員／已認可一項提案／實施自行檢測計畫／對當地河水水質）

3. People who lose their jobs/ after their house mortgage has been **approved**/ should be honest/ and explain their situation to the lenders.

（失業的人／在獲得房貸之後／應該誠實／對貸方解釋他們的狀況）

### 🌐 說明

人／機構＋accept/ approve＋人／事物（接受／認可），表示有權利或有資格的人或機構，核准或接受他人的要求或申請；approve 比較強調經過官方正式的同意程序。

### 🌐 常見用法

a）人／機構＋accept/ approve＋人／事物（如例句第一、第二句）

b）事物＋is/ are/ was/ were＋accepted/ approved＋by 人／事物（如例句第三句）

## 多益擬真測驗

_____ **1.** The proposal has been **approved** for Technology Fee funding by all the members of the advisory _____ .

     a ) committee      b ) commodity      c ) commission      d ) commodore

_____ **2.** Voters may be surprised to find out that the public transportation package they **approved** last winter is still going through the approval _____ at the state legislature.

     a ) precision      b ) precaution      c ) process      d ) prosecution

_____ **3.** The idea that the company goes into the fast food business may be **accepted** at the _____ meeting.

     a ) ballroom      b ) boat      c ) boss      d ) board

第 4-1 ～ 4-2 題，請聽簡短獨白，選擇適當的答案 🎧 ⑤

_____ **4 - 1.** What type of product does Epiphyte, Inc. make?

     a ) Software                  b ) Computers

     c ) Recording machines    d ) Fax machines

_____ **4 - 2.** Do you need work experience to apply?

     a ) A little work experience    b ) Computer experience

     c ) None whatsoever           d ) Research experience

# 句法 9

## 建議

出現機率：★★★★★

人／機構／提案 ＋ recommend/ suggest ＋ V-ing/ that（建議事項）

## 🔵 例句

1. The proposal/ **recommends**/ relocating the headquarters/ to the suburbs/ to obtain needed space.

   （企劃案／建議／重新安置總公司的地點／到郊區／以便取得需要的空間）

2. The manager/ **suggested**/ to them/ that they hold a farewell party/ for Ms. Lloyd.

   （經理／建議／對他們／舉行惜別會／為 Lloyd 女士）

3. Employees are allowed to wear casual dress/ on company premises,/ but **it is recommended**/ that you have a spare set of formal clothes on hand/ just in case.

   （員工獲准穿著便服／在辦公場所／但仍建議／在手邊有件備用的正式服裝／以防萬一）

## 🔵 說明

人／機構／提案 ＋ recommend/ suggest ＋ V-ing/ that（建議），表示對某人或機構建議該執行的事項；常出現在職場中說明公司政策或傳達規定的情境。recommend 與 suggest 句法相同，但 recommend 用在更為正式的建議事項上。

## 🔵 常見用法

a）人／機構／提案 ＋ recommend/ suggest ＋ V-ing/ 事項（如例句第一句）

b）人／機構／提案＋ recommend/ suggest ＋ that ＋ S ＋ V（如例句第二句）

如要表達對某人的建議，可用 to ＋人。

c）it is/ was ＋ recommended/ suggested that ＋ S ＋ V（如例句第三句）

it 是指後面 that ＋ S ＋ V，表示句中所建議的事項。

## 多益擬真測驗

_____ **1.** A dermatologist **suggested** placing a heat shield under the laptop to avoid the

risk of_____ if you have to hold it in your lap.

     a）falls       b）burns       c）cuts       d）scars

_____ **2.** It is highly _____ to thoroughly wash the upper part of all soda cans

before drinking out of them.

     a）recognized      b）recommended    c）contended      d）recompensed

_____ **3.** Some studies **suggest** that over the long term, if you have a choice of eating less

or exercising more, exercise will be the better _____ choice.

     a）weight-loss      b）weight-gain      c）wage-loan      d）weight-lifter

第 4-1 ～ 4-2 題，請聽簡短獨白，選擇適當的答案 🎧 26

_____ **4 - 1.** What time is this information broadcast?

     a）7:15 a.m.      b）8:00 a.m.      c）1:01 p.m.      d）8:00 p.m.

_____ **4 - 2.** How long has 101 North been closed?

     a）Not more than 15 minutes      b）Not specified

     c）All morning      d）All day

# 句法 10

## 參加;參與

出現機率：★★★★★

人 + attend/ join/ participate in + 會議 / 團體 / 活動
（出席 / 加入 / 參與）

### ● 例句

1. Practically no one in this office/ gave up the opportunity/ to **attend**/ the computer skill workshop.

（這間辦公室幾乎沒有人 / 放棄機會 / 出席 / 電腦技術研討會）

2. *The Earth is Flat* runs for 90 minutes,/ and we invite you/ to **join** us/ at the end of the movie/ for a Q-&-A session with the filmmakers.

（《地球是平的》片長 90 分鐘 / 邀請您 / 加入我們 / 在影片結束時 / 與製片人的問答時間）

3. Hazprom Inc./ would **participate in**/ the construction of the Trans-Sahara gas pipeline/ that could become a major source/ of gas supplies to Europe.

（Hazprom 公司 / 將參與 / 橫越撒哈拉沙漠的天然氣管線建造 / 可能成為主要來源 / 歐洲天然氣供應的）

### ● 說明

人 + attend/ join/ participate in + 會議 / 團體 / 活動（出席 / 加入 / 參與），這三個字都有參加的意涵，常出現在多益測驗的辦公文書及會議情境。

### ● 常見用法

a）人 + attend + 會議（如例句第一句）。attend 通常是指「人」出現在活動會場。

b）人＋ join ＋團體（如例句第二句）。join 是指加入某個特定團體，成為其中一分子。

c）人／機構＋ participate in ＋活動（如例句第三句）。participate in 是實質且積極的參與某個活動。

## 多益擬真測驗

_____ **1.** All full-time staff are _____ to **participate in** the health plan, which becomes effective on the first of May.

    a ) legible          b ) edible          c ) eligible          d ) literate

_____ **2.** Three engineers from Germany will be _____ our company for the big project next spring.

    a ) attending          b ) joining          c ) enjoining          d ) participating

_____ **3.** Since many people want to **attend** the awards ceremony on Saturday, extra buses will be made _____ to the public.

    a ) attachable          b ) available          c ) additional          d ) affordable

第 4-1 ～ 4-2 題，請聽簡短獨白，選擇適當的答案 🎧 27

_____ **4 - 1.** What is this program designed to do?

    a ) Raise money for schools.          b ) Allow adults to earn a high-school diploma.

    c ) Teach physics.          d ) Teach young people about work.

_____ **4 - 2.** How has learning changed in Castle Rock?

    a ) Children are no longer required to take algebra.

    b ) Children are getting hands-on experience.

    c ) Children are studying at home.

    d ) Local merchants are teaching classes.

# Part C

# Objects
# or Events
# 事物說明

包括對於事物本身的描述、位置、
價值、選擇、替代、比較；另外還
有對於事物的提供、利用、處理、
捐獻等。提升讀者對於事物說明的
遣詞用字能力。

# 句法 1

## 避免

## 人 / 事物 / 機構 ＋ prevent/ keep/ stop ＋ 人 / 事物 ＋ from V-ing（阻止；妨礙）

### 例句

1. Mr. Willis' insufficient experience/ in systems programming/ may **prevent** him **from**/ securing the new job.

   （Willi 先生的經驗不足 / 在系統程式設計 / 可能妨礙他 / 獲得新工作）

2. The regulations/ **keep** manufacturers **from**/ making claims/ that dietary supplements treat various diseases/ and medical conditions.

   （法規 / 阻止廠商 / 聲稱 / 膳食補充品可治療各類疾病 / 及醫療症狀）

3. In Hungary,/ the National Disaster Unit/ poured plaster into a nearby river/ to **stop** the toxic mud **from**/ flowing into the Danube.

   （在匈牙利 / 國家救災單位 / 將石灰倒入附近河川 / 以防止有毒泥漿 / 流入多瑙河）

### 說明

prevent/ keep/ stop ＋ 人 / 事物 ＋ from V-ing（阻止；妨礙），表示阻止某人做某件事情，或妨礙某件事情發生。

### 常見用法

a）人 / 事物 / 機構 ＋ prevent/ keep/ stop ＋ 人 / 事物 ＋ from V-ing

（如例句第一、例句第二句）

b）S＋V＋to prevent/ keep/ stop ＋人／事物＋from V-ing（如例句第三句）

表示藉著 S＋V 所陳述的方法，來達到阻止某事發生的目的。

## 多益擬真測驗

**1.** By downloading our CleanNet Filter, you can **stop** your mailbox **from** being _____ with spam.

   a）flooded      b）flourished      c）fluffed      d）floated

**2.** To **keep** your dog **from** pulling on the leash, wait for the dog to _____ down before opening your door and beginning the walk.

   a）fall      b）come      c）calm      d）pin

**3. Keep** yourself **from** spending money on _____ purchases by setting specific amounts for your expense categories every month.

   a）impulse      b）provocation      c）preparation      d）improvisation

第 4-1 ～ 4-2 題，請聽簡短獨白，選擇適當的答案 🎧 28

**4 - 1.** Why do most sleep apnea cases go untreated?

   a）It is an uncommon disease.      b）There is no cure.

   c）It affects too many people.      d）Most people are unaware of it.

**4 - 2.** Who can have this disease?

   a）Men      b）People who are overweight

   c）Older people      d）Anyone

# 句法 2
## 表示替代 – 1

出現機率：★★☆☆☆

---

**S ＋ V ＋ instead of/ in place of ＋ 人 / 事物 / V-ing（取代；代替）**

## ⬤ 例句

1. Holiday requests/ must be submitted/ with a minimum of four weeks notice/ **in place of**/ the usual two weeks.

   （長假的請求 / 必須提出申請 / 至少在四週以前 / 而不是 / 平常的兩週）

2. **Instead of** seeing outsourcing as a negative trend,/ it is more meaningful/ to see it as something/ that will create new opportunities/ for workers in other areas.

   （不將外包視為負面趨勢 / 更具意義的 / 看待它 / 將創造更多機會 / 給其他領域的工作者）

## ⬤ 說明

S ＋ V ＋ instead of/ in place of ＋ 人 / 事物 / V-ing（取代；代替），職場中常用在以一個方案取代另一個方案的情境。

## ⬤ 常見用法

a）S ＋ V ＋ instead of/ in place of ＋ 人 / 事物（如例句第一句）

   S ＋ V 的部分是敘述要採取的行動或方案，instead of/ in place of 後面接續的字詞是指被替代的人或事物。

b）instead of/ in place of ＋ V-ing, S ＋ V（如例句第二句）

   V-ing 指被替代的某項動作。

## 多益擬真測驗

_____ **1. Instead of** reaching for a carbonated soft drink loaded with sugar and chemicals, many people these days are looking for a natural _____ .

a) alternative      b) resource      c) perspective      d) process

_____ **2.** Using vegetable oil **in place of** diesel fuel _____ greenhouse gases and particulate pollutants.

a) introduces      b) seduces      c) deduces      d) reduces

_____ **3.** The reason why most racing cars are manual **instead of** _____ is that manual transmissions allow the driver to control the entire vehicle.

a) automatic      b) intentional      c) energetic      d) electronic

第 4 題，請聽簡短對話，選擇適當的答案 🎧 29

_____ **4.** Why has the paper NOT arrived?

a) The company ran out of paper.

b) The truck got into an accident.

c) The company is closed on Tuesdays.

d) The delivery schedule was changed.

# 句法 3
## 表示替代 – 2

出現機率：★★★☆☆

## 人 1 / 事物 1 ＋ replace ＋ 人 2 / 事物 2（1 取代或替換 2）

### ◉ 例句

1. The new trains/ will gradually **replace**/ those currently in service,/ introduced by NW Railway 25 years ago.

（新的火車 / 將逐漸替換 / 那些目前在行駛的火車 / 由 NW 鐵路公司 25 年前引進）

2. By **replacing** incandescent light bulbs/ **with** fluorescent light bulbs,/ you'll save money and help the environment.

（替換白熾燈泡 / 用日光燈管 / 省錢並且環保）

3. Ken Murphy,/ LIC Group CEO,/ will **be replaced by** Wilson Akerson,/ LIC board member.

（Ken Murphy / LIC 集團的執行長 / 將被 Wilson Akerson 取代 / 即 LIC 董事會成員）

### ◉ 說明

人 1 / 事物 1 ＋ replace ＋ 人 2 / 事物 2（1 替換 2），通常是指原先的人或事物不夠好或不堪使用，而用其他更佳的人選或新事物去替換，常見於職場的人事或公司資產情境。

### ◉ 常見用法

a）人 1 / 事物 1 ＋ replace ＋ 人 2 / 事物 2（如例句第一句）

b）人 / 機構 ＋ replace ＋ 人 2 / 事物 2 ＋ with ＋ 人 1 / 事物 1（如例句第二句）

c）人₂／事物₂＋ will be/ am/ is/ are/ was/ were ＋ replaced ＋ by/ with ＋人₁／事物₁（如
   例句第三句）

請注意：以上句法都是以 1 替換 2。

## 多益擬真測驗

_____ **1.** I am allergic to pears and tomatoes; if possible, I would like these to be
        _____ by apples in my shipment.

   a）replaced        b）complimented    c）commented     d）compared

_____ **2.** Please note that this booklet is intended as information only and does not
        **replace** or _____ the product warranty.

   a）compliment     b）comment      c）supplement       d）implement

_____ **3.** Mr. Takemi was surprised to hear that half of the computer parts were
        _____ and had to **be replaced**.

   a）detective       b）infective      c）protective        d）defective

第 4-1 ～ 4-2 題，請聽簡短獨白，選擇適當的答案 🎧 30

_____ **4 - 1.** Why are bananas recommended to athletes?

   a）They make people stronger.       b）They improve skills.

   c）They replace one's body fluids.    d）They improve speed.

_____ **4 - 2 .** Which disease does the speaker claim bananas can lower the rate of?

   a）Heart disease                     b）Flu

   c）Diabetes                          d）Cancer

# 句法 4

## 表示替代－3

出現機率：★★☆☆☆

## an alternative to ＋ 事物（對某事物的替代品或方案）

### 🔵 例句

1. Some doctors recommend laser surgery/ as **an** effective **alternative**/ **to** traditional methods of vision correction.

   （有些醫師推薦雷射手術 / 做為一種有效的替代方案 / 相對於傳統視力矯正方法）

2. There are many natural **alternatives**/ **to** synthetic sweeteners/ for mild diabetics/ and the calorie-counting eater.

   （有許多天然的替代物品 / 對於合成糖精 / 供輕微糖尿病患者 / 及計算熱量的飲食者）

### 🔵 說明

an alternative to ＋ 事物（對某事物的替代品或方案），表示對於某事物的其它選項或替代方案；此句法常出現在會議報告或產品說明情境。

### 🔵 常見用法

S ＋ V ＋ an alternative to ＋ 事物

alternative 表示對於接在其後的事物的替代方案；如例句第一句是以雷射手術作為傳統視力矯正的替代方案；例句第二句是以天然物品替代合成糖精。

## 多益擬真測驗

_____ **1.** Scientists have found that playing active video games can be a good
_____ to moderate exercise for children.

    a ) entertainment    b ) consumer      c ) alternative      d ) alternation

_____ **2.** Rural sourcing may be **an alternative to** outsourcing that can yield cost savings
while supporting _____ economic development.

    a ) regional        b ) global        c ) extensive      d ) broad

_____ **3.** An electric bike can be an exceptionally convenient and _____ **alternative
to** a car for around-town travel.

    a ) consuming     b ) cost-effective    c ) accelerating      d ) cost-free

第 4-1 ～ 4-2 題，請聽簡短獨白，選擇適當的答案 🎧 **31**

_____ **4 - 1.** Why have synthetic sweetners fallen in popularity?

    a ) Because they taste bad

    b ) Because they are expensive

    c ) Because they are out of fashion

    d ) Because they contain materials which are bad for your health

_____ **4 - 2 .** What are the natural alternatives to synthetic sweetners
derived from?

    a ) Fruits and rice             b ) Saccharin

    c ) Cane sugar               d ) Brown syrup

# 句法 5
## 描述事物 – 1

出現機率：★★★★☆

## 人／事物＋seem/ appear/ look＋修飾人或事物的字詞（看起來；似乎）

### 📖 例句

1. The technology/ applied to the car engine/ **seems** impressive;/ it cuts fuel consumption by 10 percent.

（科技／運用在汽車引擎上／看起來非常突出／它降低百分之十的耗油量）

2. The web-based courses/ **appear** to be an ideal platform/ to support higher levels of learning.

（這個以網路為基礎的課程／似乎是個理想的平台／支持進階層次的學習）

3. The streets **looked** a mess/ after Typhoon Frank swept the city.

（街道看起來一團亂／在法蘭克颱風掃過本市之後）

### 📖 說明

人／事物＋seem/ appear/ look＋修飾人或事物的字詞（看起來；似乎），常用在對於某人或某件事物的外表描述或是不太確定的推測及看法。

### 📖 常見用法

a）人／事物＋seem/ appear/ look＋修飾字詞（如例句第一句）

b）人／事物＋seem/ appear＋to be＋修飾字詞（如例句第二句）。look不適用此句法。

a）人 / 事物 ＋ seem/ look ＋ 名詞（如例句第三句）。appear 不適用此句法。

## 多益擬真測驗

_____ **1.** One brick may **seem** _____ but it is an important piece of a stable and enduring building.

　　a）authentic　　　b）insignificant　　c）substantial　　d）solid

_____ **2.** Wearing the right suit to make you **look** _____ is part of the key to a successful job interview.

　　a）compatible　　b）compact　　　c）confident　　d）unkempt

_____ **3.** When attending outdoor activities, be sure to drink plenty of liquids. If anyone **appears** to be _____ from heat exhaustion, please take them to the first aid center.

　　a）preventing　　b）sacrificing　　c）differing　　d）suffering

第 4-1 ～ 4-2 題，請聽簡短獨白，選擇適當的答案 🎧 32

_____ **4 - 1.** What suggestion has been made?

　　a）Keep the office tidy.　　　　　b）Use PCs more considerately.

　　c）Lower the volume level on the radio.　d）Walk across the room quietly.

_____ **4 - 2.** What is going to be done about the space problem?

　　a）Some desks will be thrown away.　b）Another building will be bought.

　　c）Another floor will be used.　　　d）The office layout will be changed.

# 句法 6
## 描述事物 – 2

出現機率：★★★☆☆

人 / 機構 ＋ describe/ treat/ regard ＋ 人 / 事物 ＋ as （形容為 / 看待；視為……）

### 🔵 例句

1. He **described**/ the biggest problem of buying a used car/ **as** inheriting someone else's problems.

   （他形容 / 買中古車最大的問題 / 是承接別人的問題）

2. A health research institute/ developed the concept of/ **treating** patients **as** consumers/ by rating the quality of care/ patients receive from their doctors.

   （一家健康研究機構 / 發展了一種觀念 / 視病患為顧客 / 藉著評比照護品質 / 病患從醫生接受到的）

3. Nutritionists/ **regard** green tea/ **as** one of the best sources of antioxidants.

   （營養學家 / 視綠茶 / 為最佳的抗氧化來源之一）

### 🔵 說明 ·······························································································

describe/ treat/ regard ＋ 人 / 事物 ＋ as （形容為 / 看待；視為……），describe 是指將某個人或事物形容為一種狀況；treat 及 regard 則是將某人或某物視為另一種人或事物。

🌐 **常見用法**

a）人／機構＋describe＋人／事物＋as V-ing ／人或事物（如例句第一句）

b）人／機構＋treat/ regard＋人／事物＋as 人／事物（如例句第二、三句）

## 多益擬真測驗

_____ **1.** Mayor Leonard proudly **described** the city **as** a place where the citizens are _____ for their hospitality.

　　a）notified　　　b）denounced　　　c）known　　　d）taken

_____ **2.** If you **treat** _____ **as** friends, they are more likely to become advocates for the products or services of your company.

　　a）competitors　b）customs　　c）customers　　d）custodians

_____ **3.** Analysts **regard** the percentage _____ in unemployment **as** signs of economic recovery.

　　a）decrease　　　b）decency　　c）depreciation　　d）delinquency

第 4-1 ～ 4-2 題，請聽簡短獨白，選擇適當的答案 🎧 33

_____ **4 - 1.** Why do the police think the robberies were related?

　　a）The banks were on the same street.

　　b）The same bank owned all the branches.

　　c）The robber confessed to his crimes.

　　d）The descriptions of the robber were identical.

_____ **4 - 2.** When did the robberies take place?

　　a）In the morning　　　　　b）Late at night

　　c）In the afternoon　　　　d）In the early evening

# 句法 7

## 描述事物的可得性

## access to + 設施 / 資源 / 場所（進入；進入的權利 / 通道）

### 🌐 例句

1. We provide instant **access to**/ airlines-related websites/ to give you the lowest ticket prices.

   （我們提供立即進入 / 各航空公司相關網站 / 提供您最低的票價）

2. General admission tickets/ allow **access to** all sections of the water park/ except the sauna area,/ which costs an additional $10.

   （一般入場券 / 允許進入水公園所有區域 / 除了三溫暖區域 / 要加收十元費用）

3. There will be no **access to**/ the building from the garage/ during night time;/ please use the main street entrance.

   （將沒有通道 / 從停車場進入大樓 / 在夜間 / 請利用大門的入口）

### 🌐 說明

access to + 設施 / 資源 / 場所（進入；進入的權利 / 通道），表示能夠接觸、使用某項設施或資源，或是進入某個場所的通道。

### 🌐 常見用法

a）S + V + access to + 設施 / 資源（如例句第一、第二句）。此為最常見的用法，access to 後面常接續 computer, the Internet, resources, data, service 等字彙。

b）S＋V＋access to＋場所（如例句第三句）。access 在此句法解釋為通道或入口。

## 多益擬真測驗

_____ **1.** According to the new entrance and exit regulation, lab workers need special _____ to gain **access to** the Research and Development Division.

  a）forbiddance    b）promise    c）permission    d）prestige

_____ **2.** With **access to** the road network and rail freight links, the South Eastern area of this country is an _____ place to locate production facilities.

  a）idea    b）ideal    c）identical    d）ideological

_____ **3.** _____ to ensure **access to** drinking water may expose the community to the risk of outbreaks of waterborne and infectious diseases.

  a）Failure    b）Fallacy    c）Favor    d）Fabrication

第 4-1 ～ 4-2 題，請聽簡短獨白，選擇適當的答案 🎧 34

_____ **4 - 1.** What are included in the 250,000 titles?

  a）Newspapers    b）Cassette tapes
  c）Video tapes    d）Computer discs

_____ **4 - 2.** What can you do in the computer lab?

  a）Write reports.    b）Play video games.
  c）Send e-mail.    d）Teach computer programming.

## 句法 8

### 處於某情況

出現機率：★★★☆☆

---

## 人 / 事件 ＋ place/ put ＋ 人 / 機構 ＋ under/ into/ out of ＋ 情況（置於……處境）

### 💿 例句

1. The severe recession/ has **put** a lot of companies **out of** business/ in the past ten months.

   （嚴重的經濟衰退 / 已讓許多公司倒閉 / 在過去十個月裡）

2. Many people treat credit cards/ as something useful,/ but excessive credit card debt/ can **put** them **into** a difficult situation.

   （許多人視信用卡 / 為有用的物品 / 但是過多的卡債 / 會讓他們陷入困境）

3. Once a patient **is placed under** hospice care,/ all medications related to the terminal diagnosis/ are covered by the health insurance.

   （一旦病人被納入安寧照護 / 所有與最終診療相關的醫藥 / 都由健保給付）

### 💿 說明

人 / 事件 ＋ place/ put ＋ 人 / 機構 ＋ under ＋ 情況（置於……處境），表示將某人或某機構置於某種處境下。

### 💿 常見用法

a）人 / 事件 ＋ place/ put ＋ 人 / 機構 ＋ under ＋ 情況（如例句第一、第二句）

除了 under 外，也可以用 in, into, out of 等字詞。

b）人／機構 ＋ be placed/ put ＋ under ＋ 情況（如例句第三句）

## 多益擬真測驗

_____ **1.** The judge has **placed** AnnKor Group's CEO **under** formal _____ as part of a probe into the insider-trading case.

a）investigation    b）interest     c）invention     d）investment

_____ **2.** The superstar's sudden death has **put** the _____ **under** heavy strain as millions logged on to their computers to search for related information online.

a）interface     b）Internet     c）interaction     d）interlude

_____ **3.** Accounts **placed** with a collection agency may _____ your credit history and affect your ability to establish new lines of credit for the next five years.

a）damage     b）benefit     c）decline     d）adorn

第 4-1 ～ 4-2 題，請聽簡短獨白，選擇適當的答案 🎧 ③⑤

_____ **4 - 1.** What has the store done for people who want to paint Easter eggs?

a）Moved the eggs next to the paints.

b）Moved the paints next to the egg case.

c）Put the paints on sale for 50 percent off.

d）Put the eggs on sale for $1.50 per pack.

_____ **4 - 2.** What is on sale for 50 percent off?

a）Glazed hams      b）Everything in the egg and diary case

c）All of the Easter candy     d）Some of the Easter candy

# 句法 9

## 說明條件

出現機率：★★★☆☆

---

## S₁ ＋ V₁, unless ＋ S₂ ＋ V₂（除非……）

### 🔵 例句

1. Late payment fees/ may not be more than $25/ **unless** your credit card company shows/ it incurred higher costs/ because of the late payment.

   （滯納金 / 不得超過美金 25 元 / 除非你的信用卡公司證明 / 這招致更多成本產生 / 因為延遲付款）

2. There is a $2.00 Shipping and Handling fee/ on all products/ **unless** otherwise specified.

   （運送處理費美金 2 元 / 附加在所有產品上 / 除非另行詳述）

3. **Unless** you have a reservation,/ you'll have to wait about an hour.

   （除非你有訂位 / 你將必須等候大約一個小時）

### 🔵 說明

S₁ ＋ V₁, unless ＋ S₂ ＋ V₂（除非……），表示 S₂ ＋ V₂ 所敘述的事情成立時，S₁ ＋ V₁ 所陳述的狀況就不會發生；在職場上常出現在公司政策或合約條文的內容中。

### 🔵 常見用法

a）S₁ ＋ V₁, unless ＋ S₂ ＋ V₂（如例句第一句）

b）S ＋ V, unless otherwise ＋ specified/ indicated/ noted（如例句第二句）

此句法非常普遍，最常出現在正式商業文件的規範，或是產品說明書中，表示「一種排除條款或標記」。

c ) Unless ＋ S2 ＋ V2, S1 ＋ V1（如例句第三句）

## 多益擬真測驗

_____ **1.** This plant is _____ , but **unless** it is cooked well, you will get sick.

    a ) edible      b ) illegible      c ) eligible      d ) amiable

_____ **2.** To protect the rights of credit card holder, a credit card cannot be used **unless** it is _____ from cardholder's home phone.

    a ) invalidated      b ) activated      c ) acceded      d ) cancelled

_____ **3.** The following regulations apply to all levels of tournament competition **unless** _____ specified.

    a ) other than      b ) rather than      c ) otherwise      d ) elsewhere

第 4 題，請聽簡短對話，選擇適當的答案 🎧 36

_____ **4.** When was the bill supposed to be paid?

    a ) A month ago          b ) Last week

    c ) Two weeks ago      d ) Yesterday

第 5 題，請聽簡短對話，選擇適當的答案 🎧 37

_____ **5.** Where are they likely to have dinner?

    a ) In their room          b ) At Antonio's

    c ) At a Russian restaurant      d ) At a Chinese restaurant

# 句法 10

## 附加說明

---

## 主要說明或訊息 ＋ as well as ＋ 附加說明或訊息
## （除了……還 / 不但……而且）

### ● 例句

1. Improperly grown wisdom teeth/ can cause pain in the mouth and jaw,/ **as well as** gum infections and cavities.

   （長歪的智齒 / 可能造成口腔及下顎疼痛 / 還可能會牙齦發炎及齲齒）

2. Laughter/ can improve the blood flow in your veins/ **as well as** release hormones in your brain/ that are good for your immune system.

   （大笑 / 能夠促進血液循環 / 還可以釋放腦中的賀爾蒙 / 對免疫系統有益處）

3. Every time your jingle is aired,/ your marketing message is reinforced/ **as well as** multiplied/ by your musical theme.

   （每當廣告歌曲一播送 / 行銷訊息就被強化 / 此外尚有相乘效果 / 藉著音樂主題）

### ● 說明

as well as（除了……還），表示在陳述一個事情時，附加其他說明或訊息，句子的重點在 as well as 前面的字詞；常出現在多益試題的商品說明情境。

### ● 常見用法

a ) S ＋ V ＋ N₁ ＋ as well as ＋ N₂（如例句第一句）

b ) S ＋ V₁ ＋ N₁ ＋ as well as ＋ V₂ ＋ N₂（如例句第二句）

c) S + be + Ved₁ + as well as + Ved₂（如例句第三句）

由以上可看出 as well as 前後對稱的詞性用法，這是最常出現在國際職場溝通的方式。

## 多益擬真測驗

_____ **1.** If the product has been found to be _____ , the customer should bring the product with this warranty certificate **as well as** the receipt to the place of purchase.

a ) defective      b ) perfect      c ) decent      d ) feasible

_____ **2.** A mortgage payment requires financial _____ **as well as** enough money.

a ) disciple      b ) disagreement      c ) discussion      d ) discipline

_____ **3.** If an employee can work in a team and take guidance from the other members, all the skills of the members collectively can make a difference in the quality **as well as** the _____ of the performance.

a ) quote      b ) queue      c ) quantity      d ) quad

第 4-1 ～ 4-2 題，請聽簡短獨白，選擇適當的答案 🎧 38

_____ **4 - 1.** What is Edward Richardson head of?

a ) A banking group          b ) A steel company

c ) The field of economics   d ) A medium-sized company

_____ **4 - 2.** What was Edward Richardson given an award for?

a ) His explanation of his company

b ) His excitement about politics

c ) His appearance on the show *Finance in Review*

d ) His ideas on the effects of globalization

# 句法 11

## 提供

## 人／機構＋provide＋事物／服務（提供……）

### ◉ 例句

1. Midtown Hospital/ compares favorably with other hospitals/ and **provides** services at lower rates.

（城中醫院／相較於其他醫院更有利／提供比較便宜的服務）

2. At Maxwell Fabrics,/ we always aim to/ **provide** our customers/ **with** the most competent, professional service.

（在 Maxwell 織品公司／我們一直致力／提供顧客／最滿意及專業的服務）

3. The quiet mountain setting of Riverfront Hotel/ **provides** a refreshing change/ **for** visitors/ who live in a crowded city.

（Riverfront 飯店寧靜的山中環境／提供耳目一新的改變／給造訪者／居住在擁擠的城市）

### ◉ 說明

人／機構＋provide＋事物／服務（提供……），表示某人或機構提供某種商品或服務，常出現在多益測驗的公司政策及商品說明情境中。

### ◉ 常見用法

a）人／機構＋provide＋事物／服務（如例句第一句）

b）人／機構＋provide＋提供對象＋with＋事物／服務（如例句第二句）

c）人／機構＋provide＋事物／服務＋for＋提供對象（如例句第三句）

## 多益擬真測驗

_____ **1.** If you are looking for island adventures, our concierge desk will be happy to **provide** you **with** _____ about Maui's many outdoor activities.

　　a）information　　b）informer　　c）intrigue　　d）tourist

_____ **2.** In the light of the recent financial crisis, life insurers ought to be required to **provide** customers **with** annual reports that _____ the rate of return on the policy's savings component.

　　a）conceal　　b）recover　　c）disclose　　d）close

_____ **3.** You may not want to work as a waitress or sales clerk, but these entry-level jobs **provide** the necessary stepping stones **for** you to _____ to higher positions.

　　a）progress　　b）lift　　c）increase　　d）raise

第 4-1 ～ 4-2 題，請聽簡短獨白，選擇適當的答案　🎧 **39**

_____ **4 - 1.** What is this company proud of?

　　a）Its competitive prices　　b）Its variety of rental car choices

　　c）Its nationwide business　　d）Its easy access to airports

_____ **4 - 2.** What might customers win during the campaign?

　　a）A car rental discount　　b）Airplane tickets to Los Angeles

　　c）A free stay at a luxury hotel　　d）Discount coupons for hotels

# 句法 12

## 說明事件的情況

---

## There is no doubt/ question/ evidence ＋ that ＋ S ＋ V
（無庸置疑 / 無證據顯示……）

### 🔘 例句

1. **There is no doubt**/ that the auto factory/ is expected to/ contribute to the job market/ by creating 15,000 job opportunities.

   （無庸置疑的 / 汽車工廠 / 預計會 / 對就業市場有所貢獻 / 藉由創造 15,000 個工作機會）

2. **There is no question**/ that mass-market tourism/ has put the ecologist's paradise/ in danger.

   （無庸置疑的 / 大規模的旅遊市場 / 已經讓這生態學者的天堂 / 處於險境）

3. **There is no evidence**/ to suggest/ that hormonal therapy/ protects against bone loss.

   （沒有證據 / 顯示 / 賀爾蒙療法 / 防止骨骼流失）

### 🔘 說明

There is no doubt/ question/ evidence ＋ that ＋ S ＋ V（無庸置疑 / 無證據顯示……），表示 S ＋ V 所陳述的事情是沒有疑問的或是沒有證據顯示其為真實的；常出現在多益試題的商務行銷或科技的情境。

### 🔘 常見用法

a ) There is no doubt/ question/ evidence ＋ that ＋ S ＋ V（如例句第一、第二句）

b ) There is no evidence ＋ to-V（如例句第三句）

evidence 後 面 常 接 續 的 不 定 式 動 詞（to-V） 包 括 to suggest, to indicate, to support，表示沒有證據「顯示／指出／支持」某個事情或論述。

## 多益擬真測驗

_____ **1.** There is no _____ that GM crops and food made from them are toxic or allergenic.

a ) evidence      b ) program      c ) assistant      d ) access

_____ **2. There is no doubt** that these fitness programs _____ the importance of an active lifestyle and encourage community involvement.

a ) highlight      b ) force      c ) require      d ) plead

_____ **3. There is no evidence** to _____ that the use of mobile phones or laptops was the cause of the latest aviation safety incident.

a ) express      b ) digest      c ) suggest      d ) protrude

第 4-1 〜 4-2 題，請聽簡短獨白，選擇適當的答案 🎧 40

_____ **4 - 1.** Why have the people listening been gathered?

a ) To be tried for criminal charges      b )To be selected for some duty

c ) To select representatives of the jury      d ) To learn about the history of juries

_____ **4 - 2.** What will they do after this speech?

a ) Introduce themselves.      b ) Register to vote.

c ) Write essays.      d ) Answer a series of questions.

# Part D

# Operations
# 商務運作

介紹商務運作的五大要素：目的、
金錢、時間、原因、事物發展，不
但提供完整具體的專業表達方式，
讓讀者熟悉一般商務運作的架構。

# 句法 1

## 表達可能性

出現機率：★★☆☆☆

## There is a possibility ＋ that/ of/ to V（有……可能性）

### 📙 例句

1. **There is a possibility**/ that the committee will approve a bankruptcy plan/ and resolve to file legal claims/ against Tri-Speed Co.

   （有可能 / 委員會將批准破產計劃 / 並決議提出索賠 / 對 Tri-Speed 公司）

2. According to the data provided,/ **there is a possibility** of/ acquiring intra-hospital infection.

   （根據所提供的資料 / 有可能是 / 得到院內感染）

3. The analysis indicates/ that **there is a possibility**/ to cut costs/ by streamlining the production process.

   （分析顯示 / 有可能 / 降低成本 / 藉著提高生產製程的效率）

### 📙 說明

There is a possibility ＋ that/ of/ to V（有……可能性），表示某種可能性的存在，常用於推測事情的原因或後續發展。

### 📙 常見用法

a) There is a possibility ＋ that ＋ S ＋ V（如例句第一句）

b) There is a possibility ＋ of ＋ V-ing/ 事物（如例句第二句）

c) There is a possibility ＋ to-V（如例句第三句）

## 多益擬真測驗

_____ **1.** Residents living in a low-lying area are preparing for an _____ , because **there is a possibility** of dike collapse.

a ) exhibition     b ) explanation     c ) exemption     d ) evacuation

_____ **2. There is a possibility** of hair getting caught in a moving portion of the line, so _____ must be worn at all times near the assembly line.

a ) hair extensions     b ) hair sprays     c ) hair nets     d ) hair styles

_____ **3.** As structures become more air-tight and interior materials become more synthetic, **there is a possibility** that the indoor air quality is _____.

a ) deteriorating     b ) increasing     c ) progressing     d ) improving

第 4-1 ～ 4-2 題，請聽簡短對話，選擇適當的答案

_____ **4 - 1.** What conclusion does the speaker make? 🎧 41

a ) That society is made to think about morality

b ) That young people always make good decisions

c ) That public scandals don't affect young people

d ) That scandals involving teen idols are bad for morality

_____ **4 - 2.** What has the incident forced society to think about?

a ) The effect of famous people on the morals of society

b ) The lack of effect on young people as a whole

c ) The popularity of teen idol Shawn Holland

d ) How many people really think about teen idols every day

# 句法 2
致力於

出現機率：★☆☆☆☆

## 人 / 機構 ＋ am/ is/ are/ was/ were ＋ committed to ＋ 事物 / V-ing（致力於某事）

### 例句

1. E C Company/ **is committed to**/ the personal growth of all employees/ through education.

   （EC 公司 / 致力於 / 所有員工的個人成長 / 經由教育訓練）

2. The Government/ **is committed to**/ minimizing the burdens on employers/ and simplifying the process for them.

   （政府 / 致力於 / 讓雇主的負擔減低到最小 / 並為他們簡化流程）

### 說明

committed to ＋ 事物（致力於某事），表示將心力專注在某件事物的達成，常用於企業宣揚理念或目標時的正式用語。

### 常見用法

a）人 / 機構 ＋ am/ is/ are/ was/ were ＋ committed to ＋ 事物（如例句第一句）

b）人 / 機構 ＋ am/ is/ are/ was/ were ＋ committed to ＋ V-ing（如例句第二句）

### 類似用法

人 / 機構 ＋ am/ is/ are/ was/ were ＋ dedicated to ＋ 事物（致力於某事）

Every member of the Decas team/ **is dedicated to**/ a customer-intimate approach to business.

（Decas 團隊的每位成員 / 都致力於 / 親近客戶的商業手法）

## 多益擬真測驗

_____ **1.** LLC Ltd. **is committed to** providing the type of products and services that deliver the highest level of performance while _____ quality and affordability.

    a ) sacrificing    b ) compensating   c ) maintaining    d ) charging

_____ **2.** If you **are committed to** _____ a career in acting, you must first have the passion and drive to learn your craft.

    a ) pursuing    b ) pursuit       c ) proposing    d ) pursued

_____ **3.** Spine Align **is committed to** the _____ of high-quality innovative medical devices for the treatment of spinal disorders.

    a ) destruction    b ) development   c ) divine      d ) derision

第 4 題，請聽簡短對話，選擇適當的答案 🎧 **42**

_____ **4.** Why is the man's friend learning Portuguese?

    a ) Because she wants to travel and aid people in need

    b ) Because she wants to travel and be a linguist

    c ) Because she wants to help people in her native country

    d ) Because she wants to teach Portuguese and help children

# 句法 3
## 表示目的 – 1

出現機率：★★★☆☆

## In order to ＋ V, S ＋ V（為了什麼目的……）

### 🔵 例句

1. **In order to** place a call outside the office,/ you have to dial zero first.

（要撥打外線電話 / 你必須先撥 0）

2. A local steel plant/ has purchased the riverfront lot/ **in order to** increase its production capacity.

（一家本地的鋼鐵廠 / 已經購置濱河區的土地 / 為了增加它的產能）

### 🔵 說明

in order to（為了……），表示為了達到某種目標的正式用語。

### 🔵 常見用法

a）In order to ＋ V, S ＋ V（如例句第一句）

把目標說明放前面，達到目標的方式放後面。

b）S ＋ V ＋ in order to ＋ 動詞（如例句第二句）

將達到目標的方式放前面，後面再接續說明想達到的目的。

## 多益擬真測驗

_____ **1. In order to** drive more _____ to his blog, Nick decides to make comments on other blogs.

 a ) Internet　　　 b ) mention　　　 c ) traffic　　　 d ) speculation

_____ **2. In order to** _____ your account online, you must set a password for your Master Username.

 a ) open　　　 b ) activate　　　 c ) interrupt　　　 d ) introduce

_____ **3.** We must implement some meaningful solutions **in order to** _____ oil consumption in our daily lives.

 a ) produce　　　 b ) reduce　　　 c ) seduce　　　 d ) induce

第 4-1 ～ 4-2 題，請聽簡短獨白，選擇適當的答案 🎧 43

_____ **4 - 1.** How long will this course take?

 a ) A few hours　　　　　　　 b ) A few days

 c ) A few weeks　　　　　　　 d ) A few months

_____ **4 - 2.** What is the purpose of the course?

 a ) To become an expert in scuba equipment

 b ) To learn to dive in any type of weather

 c ) To learn to scuba dive in safety

 d ) To learn to scuba dive cooperatively

# 句法 4
## 表示目的－2

**the aim/ intention/ purpose ＋ is/ was ＋ to V（目的是做……）**

## 🔵 例句

1. With its assets doubled/ in the past three years,/ GD Bank's **aim** is/ to proceed with its IPO next year. (IPO: initial public offering)

   （由於它的資產倍增／在過去三年／GD銀行的目標是／在明年進行它的初次公開發行）

2. The **intention** of the foundation is/ to create successful models of innovation /which can be replicated/ locally and nationally.

   （基金會的目的是／創造成功的創新模式／能夠被複製／在本地及全國）

3. The **purpose** of this activity is/ to give employees the opportunity/ to improve their cardiovascular endurance.

   （本活動的目的是／提供員工機會／增進他們心肺耐力）

## 🔵 說明

the aim/ intention/ purpose ＋ is/ was ＋ to V（目的是做……），在職場中用來表達公司的計畫目標，或是某個事件或活動的目的，最常出現在會議或活動說明等正式文件上。

## 🔵 常見用法

the aim/ intention/ purpose ＋ is/ was ＋ to V

通常會在 aim/ intention/ purpose 等字彙前面加上如 its, my, our, their 或是在後面加上 of the company/ event/ activity 等字串，來表示「誰的」目的或意圖。

## 多益擬真測驗

_____ **1.** The _____ of this assignment is to assist you in applying the various models pertaining to the psychology of stress.

    a ) agenda      b ) comment      c ) purpose      d ) dilemma

_____ **2.** The **aim** of the _____ is to determine how serious the oil spill is and to detect the composition of the oil in order to contain it in the right way.

    a ) investment      b ) integration      c ) investigation      d ) interrogation

_____ **3.** The **intention** of this paper is to _____ the truth behind the various natural ways that can cure leukemia.

    a ) discover      b ) open      c ) conceal      d ) fabricate

第 4-1 ～ 4-2 題，請聽簡短獨白，選擇適當的答案 🎧 44

_____ **4 - 1.** What is the purpose of an extra-wide wheelbase?

    a ) Speed      b ) Stability      c ) Fashion      d ) Durability

_____ **4 - 2.** What brings about the impressive power of this truck?

    a ) Pure practicality

    b ) A durable one-ton body

    c ) A 4-wheel drive system and 4-liter engine

    d ) An ingeniously designed driving unit

# 句法 5

## 計價

出現機率：★★★★★

---

## charge ＋費用＋ on sth. ／ charge ＋人＋ for sth.（記帳／索價）

### 例句

1. According to POS card loss protection plan,/ you will be covered overseas/ if you **charge** your full travel fares/ **on** your POS credit card.

（根據 POS 卡片遺失保護計劃／你在國外將得到保障／如果您將全額旅費記帳／在您的 POS 信用卡上）

2. The foreign travelers/ complained to the consumer protection agency/ after Red River Hotel **charged** them 100 dollars/ **for** the loss of a room key.

（外國旅客／對消費者保護局抱怨／在紅河飯店對他們索價一百元後／因為遺失一把房間鑰匙）

---

### 說明

charge 這個字當作動詞使用時，主要解釋為記帳及索價，最常出現於商務情境。

---

### 常見用法

a）人／機構 ＋ charge ＋ 費用項目 ＋ on ＋ 信用卡／帳戶（如例句第一句）

b）人／機構 ＋ charge ＋ 人（＋ 金額）＋ for ＋ 事物（如例句第二句）

## 多益擬真測驗

_____ **1.** EBK Airlines will _____ overweight passengers for two seats, or they may not be permitted to board their flight.

    a ) pay            b ) increase        c ) charge       d ) cost

_____ **2.** The County Toll Road Authority will **charge** carpool passengers a _____ toll of $2.50 to reduce road congestion.

    a ) appreciated     b ) raised       c ) discerned     d ) discounted

_____ **3.** People are more likely to make a purchase in a hotel if they are offered the opportunity to **charge** it to their room _____.

    a ) account       b ) accord       c ) access      d ) acceptance

第 4 題，請聽問題，選擇適當的回應 🎧 45

_____ **4.** Mark your answer on the answer sheet.

第 5 題，請聽問題，選擇適當的回應 🎧 46

_____ **5 .** Mark your answer on the answer sheet.

## 句法 6
### 商品發行

---

## 人 / 機構 ＋ launch/ start/ introduce ＋ 產品 / 事業 / 活動（開啟 / 開創 / 引進）

### 🌑 例句

1. With an eye on/ the future computer market for children,/ JMD Technology decided/ to **launch** a line of inexpensive notebook PCs.

（著眼於 / 未來兒童電腦市場 / JMD 科技公司決定 / 開啟平價筆電產品線）

2. The checklist below/ provides the basic steps/ you should follow to **start** a business.

（以下清單 / 提供基本步驟 / 你創業應遵循的）

3. Vista Coffee/ will **introduce** three new tea-based lattes/ as part of a push/ to offer customers more choices.

（Vista 咖啡公司 / 將引進三種新的以茶為基底的拿鐵 / 作為促銷 / 提供客戶更多選擇）

### 🌑 說明

launch/ start/ introduce ＋ 產品 / 事業 / 活動（開啟 / 開創 / 引進），常用於表達開啟、開創及引進新事業或產品。launch 特別是指開啟一項重要的產品或活動，通常會公開宣稱，讓大眾知道。

### 🌑 常見用法

a）人 / 機構 ＋ launch ＋ 產品 / 事業 / 活動（如例句第一句）

b ) 人／機構 ＋ start ＋ 產品／事業／活動（如例句第二句）

c ) 人／機構 ＋ introduce ＋ 產品／事業／活動（如例句第三句）

## 多益擬真測驗

_____ **1.** Some famous cancer survivors are set to **launch** a _____ foundation to give financial aid to high-risk women who can't receive timely medical treatment.

    a ) charity      b ) seminar      c ) draft      d ) campaign

_____ **2.** Mason Travel Co. **introduced** a cheap Asian _____ for the holiday season, and other travel agencies followed suit.

    a ) transportation    b ) transmission    c ) tour    d ) vogue

_____ **3.** The Medical Syndicate **launched** a campaign _____ smoking through raising awareness of its harmful effects.

    a ) for      b ) against      c ) during      d ) on

第 4-1 ～ 4-2 題，請聽簡短獨白，選擇適當的答案 🎧 **47**

_____ **4 - 1.** When is the party going to be held?

    a ) Seven days before Christmas      b ) On Christmas Eve

    c ) In a week      d ) On December 22

_____ **4 - 2.** Why is this party going to be held?

    a ) To celebrate New Year's

    b ) To liven up the neighborhood

    c ) To strengthen bonds among members

    d ) To collect money to benefit children

# 句法 7

## 持續、維持

出現機率：★★★★☆

## S ＋ stay/ remain/ keep ＋ 修飾或形容主詞的字詞（保持；仍是）

### 🔵 例句

1. If you are in an auto accident,/ please **stay** calm,/ report the accident to the police,/ and contact your insurance representative/ as soon as possible.

（如果你置身車禍現場／請保持冷靜／向警方報案／聯絡你的保險業務員／盡快）

2. Mozart,/ the most naturally-gifted musician,/ **remains** the chief attraction/ for travelers to Salzburg, Austria.

（莫札特／最具天賦的音樂家／仍然是主要的吸引力／對造訪奧地利薩爾茲堡的遊客）

3. Nassau County Police Department/ **kept** traffic moving/ during the road construction/ by implementing a comprehensive traffic management plan.

（Nassau 郡警察局／保持交通順暢／在道路施工期間／藉著執行完善的交通管理計劃）

### 🔵 說明

S ＋ stay/ remain/ keep ＋ 修飾或形容主詞的字詞（保持；仍是），表達人或事物沒有變化的狀態。

### 🔵 常見用法

a) S ＋ stay/ remain/ keep ＋ 形容字詞（如例句第一句）

b) S ＋ stay/ remain ＋ 名詞（如例句第二句），keep 不適用此句法。

c) S ＋ keep ＋ 人 / 事物 ＋ V-ing / 形容字詞（如例句第三句）

## 多益擬真測驗

_____ **1.** Conservatives predict that the financial condition of this company will **remain** _____ during the period of investigation.

a ) authoritative     b ) summarized     c ) examined     d ) stable

_____ **2. Keeping** employees _____ is something positive that any organization can do.

a ) discouraged     b ) monotonous     c ) motivated     d ) moved

_____ **3.** A reminder to you all to **stay** _____ to NPR News for updates on the earthquake situation in Haiti throughout today and tomorrow.

a ) cool     b ) awake     c ) tuned     d ) petrified

第 4-1 ～ 4-3 題，請聽簡短獨白，選擇適當的答案 🎧 **48**

_____ **4 - 1.** Where is this talk most likely taking place?

a ) On an amusement ride     b ) In an airplane

c ) On a cruise ship     d ) In a tropical area

_____ **4 - 2.** How long will the current situation continue?

a ) It is not known.     b ) For a short time

c ) For hours     d ) Until the storm stops

_____ **4 - 3.** What must the listeners do?

a ) Sit down.     b ) Fasten people in.

c ) Stop serving meals.     d ) Assist the speaker.

# 句法 8
## 說明因果－1

出現機率：★★★★☆

## due to ＋ 原因（由於某原因）

### 🔵 例句

1. The success of the project/ is/ **due to**/ the effort invested by the task force members.
   （專案的成功 / 是 / 由於 / 專案小組成員投入的努力）
2. **Due to**/ the popularity of the performer,/ theater patrons are advised to/ contact the box office as soon as possible.
   （由於 / 該表演者很受歡迎 / 劇院的觀眾被建議 / 盡快與售票處聯繫）

### 🔵 說明

due to（由於），due to 後面加上原因，用來說明導致句中後果的理由。如第一句說明專案成功的原因，第二句解釋及早購票的理由。

### 🔵 常見用法

a）事情的結果 ＋ is/ are/ was/ were ＋ due to ＋ 原因
   （正規用法，如例句第一句）
b）Due to ＋ 原因，S ＋ V
   （通俗用法，但在國際溝通中常見，如例句第二句）

## 多益擬真測驗

_____ **1.** Employees who use the gym are more relaxed, productive and spend fewer days away from work **due to** _____ .

    a ) happiness      b ) regularity      c ) illness      d ) exercise

_____ **2. Due to** time _____ , employees in Asia and South America will have to come to work outside of regular business hours.

    a ) equation      b ) difference      c ) currency      d ) fluency

_____ **3. Due to** _____ weather conditions, California has an advantage in the production of fruits and vegetables.

    a ) useful      b ) detrimental      c ) favorable      d ) valuable

第 4-1 ～ 4-2 題，請聽簡短獨白，選擇適當的答案 🎧 49

_____ **4 - 1.** Why is this announcement being made?

    a ) To announce a landing delay due to an accident

    b ) To announce a landing delay due to bad weather

    c ) To announce that the plane is about to descend

    d ) To announce that meals are going to be served

_____ **4 - 2.** Which is the correct description of the situation on the plane?

    a ) All passengers are probably in their seats.      b ) Electricity has been turned off.

    c ) All passengers are probably confused.      d ) Flight attendants are in the aisles.

# 句法 9

## 說明因果－2

出現機率：★★★★☆

## S ＋ V ＋ because of/ owing to/ thanks to ＋ 原因（由於 / 幸好……）

### 💿 例句

1. The Chichen Ruins/ are the most visited attraction here/ **because of** their vicinity to the tourist resort.

（Chichen 遺跡 / 是這裡遊客最常造訪的勝地 / 因為它鄰近觀光度假區）

2. **Owing to** the growing elderly population,/ the demand for health services/ is increasing year by year.

（因為逐漸成長的老年人口 / 對健康服務的需求 / 逐年增長）

3. **Thanks to** new taxes and fees imposed last year,/ the health plan's finances/ have stabilized for the moment.

（幸好去年課徵的新稅及費用 / 健保的財務狀況 / 此刻已經穩定了）

### 🔘 說明

because of/ owing to/ thanks to ＋ 原因（由於 / 幸好……），都是用來表達原因的字詞（表示歸功於……），較明顯的區別在於：thanks to 較常強調正面的事由，並因而產生好的結果；because of 及 owing to 可以接續正面或負面的原因，重點在於客觀事實的陳述。

## 常見用法

a）S＋V＋ because of/ owing to/ thanks to ＋原因（如例句第一句）

because of/ owing to/ thanks to 放在句尾，S＋V 則說明結果。

b）because of/ owing to/ thanks to ＋原因，S＋V（如例句第二及第三句）

because of/ owing to/ thanks to 也可以放在句首，先說明原因。

## 多益擬真測驗

_____ **1.** Some students were not able to adjust the template to suit their needs, perhaps _____ a lack of skill or practice in using templates or the technology itself.

　　a ) because　　　b ) owing to　　　c ) thanks to　　　d ) due

_____ **2.** In 1983, Peter Wold founded an art community that was _____ **thanks to** a new generation of talented young artists, committed gallery owners and cultural institutions.

　　a ) decaying　　　b ) challenging　　　c ) competing　　　d ) flourishing

_____ **3. Owing to** the poor business showing, the shareholders of Hobson Motors Co. didn't get much in _____.

　　a ) diversions　　　b ) dividends　　　c ) divinations　　　d ) divisions

第 4 題，請聽簡短獨白，選擇適當的答案 🎧 50

_____ **4.** What has happened to interest in healthy food in the past 20 years?

　　a ) It has slowly dwindled.

　　b ) It has stayed pretty much the same.

　　c ) It has become irrelevant.

　　d ) It has expanded greatly.

# 句法 10
## 說明因果 – 3

## 人 / 機構 ＋ attribute 結果 ＋ to 原因（歸因於……）

### ◉ 例句

1. Some of the most successful people in the world/ **attribute** their achievements **to**/ writing down their goals/ and reviewing them daily.

   （世界上非常成功的人 / 將他們的成就歸功於 / 寫下目標 / 同時每天檢視這些目標）

2. Police/ **attributed** the car accident/ not only **to** the dense fog/ but also **to** Marie's inexperienced driving.

   （警方 / 將車禍歸因於 / 不僅是濃霧 / 而且是 Marie 駕駛經驗不足）

3. The profit decline/ was mainly **attributed to**/ a drop in prices/ and lower gross margins.

   （利潤下降 / 主要歸因於 / 價格下跌 / 及較少的毛利）

### ◉ 說明

人 / 機構 ＋ attribute 結果 ＋ to 原因（歸因於……），表示「人 / 機構」將某個結果歸因於某項因素。

### ◉ 常見用法

a）人 / 機構 ＋ attribute 結果 ＋ to 原因（如例句第一、例句第二句）

　　attribute 可以用於正面（例句第一句），也可以用於負面的事情（例句第二句）。

b）結果 ＋ be attributed to ＋ 原因（如例句第三句）

## 多益擬真測驗

_____ **1.** Employees **attribute** the low turnover rate **to** Ms. Boleyn's _____ leadership qualities.

    a ) auspicious      b ) notorious      c ) outraging      d ) outstanding

_____ **2.** Officials **attribute** the _____ in service **to** a software upgrade that makes the system run more smoothly.

    a ) improvement      b ) lift      c ) raise      d ) relocation

_____ **3.** Most of the homebuilder companies **attributed** the _____ performance by the housing industry **to** an unstable economy and less availability of credit among potential buyers.

    a ) promising      b ) probable      c ) poor      d ) illuminating

第 4-1 ～ 4-2 題，請聽簡短獨白，選擇適當的答案 🎧 51

_____ **4 - 1.** Who is likely giving this advice?

    a ) A mechanic          b ) A driving student

    c ) A radio DJ          d ) A car designer

_____ **4 - 2.** When do drivers need to remember "S-M-O-G"?

    a ) When driving in reverse

    b ) When they are on dirt roads

    c ) When changing lanes

    d ) When they are parking

## 原因 ＋ result in/ lead to ＋ 結果（促成／導致）

### ◉ 例句

1. Rather than trying to treat a chronic disease/ that has already done its damage,/ controlling it/ can **result in**/ greater longevity and happier lives.

（不是試圖去治療慢性疾病／已經造成傷害／而是去控制它／可以促成／更長壽及快樂的生活）

2. Analysts said/ the debt rating downgrade of SmartTech/ would **lead to**/ a more general pessimism regarding the telecomm industry as a whole.

（分析師說／ SmartTech 債信評等降低／將導致／對電信產業全面悲觀）

### ◉ 說明

原因 ＋ result in/ lead to ＋ 結果（促成／導致），表示某種原因促成或導致某個結果，在職場中常出現在市場分析的報告或相關文件中。

### ◉ 常見用法

a）原因 ＋ result in/ lead to ＋ 結果（促成／導致）

b）result in/ lead to 可以用於正面的敘述（如例句第一句），也可以用在負面的內容（如例句第二句）。

多益擬真測驗

_____ **1.** _____ in McWicky Company's receipt of up to $90 million of accounts receivable will **result in** a decrease of business cash flow.

a ) Punctualities    b ) Regularities    c ) Delays    d ) Protections

_____ **2.** High-fidelity medical simulations can complement medical education in patient care settings and **lead to** _____ learning.

a ) effective    b ) affective    c ) selective    d ) motive

_____ **3.** Intensive _____ of gum disease may **result in** improved blood flow and significantly reduces inflammation in the body.

a ) ignorance    b ) movement    c ) treatment    d ) assortment

第 4-1 ～ 4-2 題，請聽簡短獨白，選擇適當的答案 🎧 52

_____ **4 - 1.** According to the talk, what should one plan for before an interview?

a ) Adding experience to your resume    b ) Getting the greatest benefit from it

c ) Evading the interviewer    d ) Being talkative at the interview

_____ **4 - 2.** According to this talk, how should one answer questions?

a ) With only the truth

b ) However you please

c ) With what the interviewer wants to hear

d ) With a "yes" or a "no"

# 句法 12
## 說明因果 – 5

## 原因 ＋ account for/ explain ＋ 結果（說明 / 解釋）

### 📀 例句

1. *Daily Mail* reported/ that some lifestyle choices/ may **account for**/ the majority of strokes,/ such as smoking, alcohol consumption, poor diet, and lack of exercise.

（《每日郵報》報導／一些生活型態的選擇／可以說明／大部分中風的原因／例如吸菸、飲酒、不良飲食、及缺乏運動）

2. The lower real interest rates,/ high loan-to-value levels/ and permissive mortgage approvals/ may **explain**/ the housing bubble.

（較低的實質利率／高額房貸／及寬鬆的核貸／可以解釋／房市泡沫）

3. Sexism/ only partially **explains**/ the wage gap/ between male and female physicians.

（性別歧視／只能部分解釋／薪資差異／男性與女性醫師間的）

### 📀 說明

原因 ＋ account for/ explain ＋ 結果（說明 / 解釋），用來說明造成某個結果的原因，通常是對某個經濟現象、某種病症或是某種行為，做出較為客觀及完整的解說；常出現在商業、科技分析的報告中。

### 📀 常見用法

a）原因 ＋ account for/ explain ＋ 結果（如例句第一、第二句）

b）原因 ＋ 修飾字詞 ＋ account for/ explain ＋ 結果（如例句第三句）

## 多益擬真測驗

_____ **1.** The recession and service _____ by airlines that stopped flying on some routes may **account for** the decrease of the number of passengers in 2008.

     a ) connections     b ) interventions     c ) interruptions     d ) interludes

_____ **2.** Auto defects **account for** at least 10 percent of vehicle _____ each year, according to the Center for Auto Safety.

     a ) failures        b ) fertilizers       c ) fabrics       d ) fatalities

_____ **3.** A rise in the price of heating oil may **explain** the recent _____ noted in the operating fund.

     a ) recessions      b ) reductions      c ) rebounds      d ) rebuffs

第 4-1 ～ 4-2 題，請聽簡短獨白，選擇適當的答案

_____ **4 - 1.** What does Mr. Holcomb's company do?

     a ) It makes graphics for Websites.     b ) It does market research.

     c ) It designs ceramic products.      d ) It trains ceramic artists.

_____ **4 - 2.** Which statement is true about Mr. Holcomb's company?

     a ) It developed over a short period.

     b ) It changed the industry.

     c ) It invested $19 million in new products.

     d ) It struggled financially.

# 句法 13
## 表示事物發展

## 人／事物 + become/ grow/ turn + 形容字詞（變成；成為）

### 🌐 例句

1. Mobile phones/ have **become** so popular/ that telecommunications companies are establishing service/ in areas/ previously thought too remote.

（行動電話／已經如此普遍／以至於電信公司建置服務／在一些地區／之前被視為太偏遠）

2. Over the course of the next thirty years/ the citrus industry in Maricopa County/ will **grow to be** one of the largest in the country.

（再經過三十年／ Maricopa 郡的柑橘類水果產業／將成為全國規模最大之一）

3. There are certain medications/ that can cause the teeth/ to **turn** gray.

（有些特定的藥物／會導致牙齒／變灰色）

### 🌐 說明

人／事物 + become/ grow/ turn + 形容字詞（變成；成為），都是表示經過一段時間後，人或事物產生變化的情形；become 是較為普遍的用字，grow 特別用來表示緩慢、逐漸的變化，turn 通常用在顏色的改變。

### 🌐 常見用法

a）人／事物 + become + 形容字詞／名詞（如例句第一句）。

become 後面可以接形容字詞或名詞。

b）人／事物 ＋ grow to be ＋名詞（如例句第二句）

　　grow 後面可接形容字詞，或是接 to be ＋名詞。

c）人／事物 ＋ turn ＋ 形容字詞（如例句第三句）

## 多益擬真測驗

_____ **1.** Word has reached the fourth floor that some employees fear that because of service cutbacks, they may **become** _____ right before Christmas.

　　a ) dissatisfied　　　b ) unemployed　　　c ) classified　　　d ) unaccounted

_____ **2.** To use your hotel room card key, simply slide the card into the slot on the door handle; when the red LED **turns** green, you can open the door and _____ the room.

　　a ) leave　　　　　b ) join　　　　　　c ) enter　　　　　d ) sneak

_____ **3.** A & M Art Ltd., founded in 1990, quickly **grew** _____ and became the largest website design firm in this country.

　　a ) conspicuous　　b ) audacious　　　c ) obvious　　　　d ) prosperous

第 4-1 ～ 4-2 題，請聽簡短獨白，選擇適當的答案 🎧 54

_____ **4 - 1.** How is this company's business going to change?

　　a ) It is going out of business next month.　b ) It is changing its product line.

　　c ) It is opening a new chain of stores.　　　d ) It is being absorbed by another firm.

_____ **4 - 2.** What will be different from next month?

　　a ) Medical coverage　　　　　　b ) Working hours

　　c ) Rules about clothing　　　　　d ) Number of jobs

# TOEIC
# 900

題解

II

# Texts
# 書信與公文

# 題解 1

## 1.

**答案：** c ) survey（調查）

**中譯：** 根據《科技雜誌》的一項調查，近三年來社會的寬頻科技已快速的普及化。

　　　 a ) 規則　　　　　 b ) 政策　　　　　 c ) 調查　　　　　 d ) 聚會

**題解：** 從 conduct（執行） 以及後面的結論可推斷出應為調查或訪問，因此選項 c ) survey（調查），最符合文意。

## 2.

**答案：** b ) significantly（顯著地）

**中譯：** 根據報告指出，隨著颶風的頻率和強度不斷增加，全球暖化帶來的影響將可更明顯地感受到。

　　　 a ) 邪惡地　　　　 b ) 顯著地　　　　 c ) 大概　　　　　 d ) 深刻地

**題解：** 從 felt（感受）以及颶風的明顯改變可判斷出空格應填有強調感受程度的修飾字詞，因此選項 b ) significantly（顯著地） 最符合文意。

## 3.

**答案：** a ) regulations（規定）

**中譯：** 依據 EB 的航空安檢規定，拒絕接受全身 X 光掃描的乘客將會被禁止登機。

a）規定　　　　b）修理人員　　　c）重複　　　　d）排演

**題解**：因為是強制性的檢查，所以只有選項 a）regulations（規定）最符合文意。

# 4 - 1. ～ 4 - 2.

**聽力原文：**

This is becoming an all too familiar sight in El Paso: a smashed mailbox. It's the work of thieves looking for money in your mail. Right now, El Paso leads the nation in mail theft. Postal inspectors say drugs are the reason why. According to Postmaster Antonio Alvarez, the majority of the mail thieves they have arrested so far have been drug addicts.

To fight back, the postal service in El Paso has brought in extra inspectors. And postal workers are unveiling a new public service campaign. It's designed to educate the public about the growing mail theft problem. El Paso's Postmaster says most people are surprised when their mail turns up missing. He advises you pick up your mail regularly, use security checks and mail your bill payments at the post office or at a blue mailbox. Inspectors warn anyone caught stealing mail faces a hefty fine and jail time.

**原文翻譯：**

在 El Paso 看到毀損的信箱已經司空見慣了。那是想在信件中找錢的竊賊所犯。El Paso 現今的郵件竊賊量高居不下。郵件審查員認為毒品是一大關鍵。依照郵政總長 Antonio Alvarez 所說，至今所逮捕的郵件竊賊大多是毒癮者。

為了反擊犯罪，El Paso 開始增加審查員人力。郵政人員也開始推行新的公眾服務宣導，旨在教育大眾日益嚴重的郵件竊賊問題。El Paso 的郵政總長宣稱多數人會很訝異自己的郵件遺失。他建議大家定期收信，執行安檢並利用郵局或郵筒寄送帳單款項。審查員警告任何竊取郵件的現行犯都會面臨極重的罰款和刑期。

## 4 - 1.

答案：c）They are drug users.（他們為毒癮者）。

中譯：多數的郵件竊賊都有什麼共通處？

　　　a）他們都在郵局工作。　　　　　　b）他們都沒有固定住址。

　　　c）他們都吸毒。　　　　　　　　　d）他們都很訝異郵件遺失。

題解：第一段最後提到 ...have been drug addicts（都是毒癮者）... 所以可以得知共通處是
　　　c）They are drug users.（他們都吸毒）。

## 4 - 2.

答案：a）Brought in more postal inspectors.（引進更多郵件審查員。）

中譯：郵局做了什麼來打擊犯罪？

　　　a）引進更多郵件審查員。　　　　　b）鎖上所有信箱。

　　　c）增加犯人的罰款和刑期。　　　　d）向客戶介紹特殊的服務。

題解：第二段一開始就提到 To fight back, the postal service in El Paso has brought in
　　　extra inspectors. 因此可得知答案是 a）Brought in more postal inspectors.（引進更
　　　多郵件審查員。）

## 題解 2

**1.**

**答案**：c ) Whether（是否）

**中譯**：White 先生的生意是否能成功，取決於他的努力和運氣。

    a ) 假如          b ) 什麼          c ) 是否          d ) 哪一個

**題解**：由 depend on（取決於……）可判斷出努力和運氣是 White 先生是否能成功的關鍵，因此選 c ) Whether（是否）。

**2.**

**答案**：b ) One major concern（一個重要的考量）

**中譯**：至少對經歷過去年森林大火的小鎮居民來說，主要的考量之一是冬季的乾旱是否會持續到夏季。

    a ) 一次重要的考量          b ) 一個重要的考量

    c ) 一次考量的重要性          d ) 一個考量的重要性

**題解**：從文意中得知乾旱問題是居民考量的重點之一，所以選項 b ) One major concern（一個重要的考量）最符合文意。

**3.**

**答案**：b ) decision（決定）

**中譯：**澳洲的運動員必須自行決定是否參加在新德里的大英國協運動會，該區目前仍是旅遊警戒範圍。

a ) 投資　　　　　b ) 決定　　　　　c ) 精確　　　　　d ) 奚落

**題解：**make one's own decision（自行做決定）因此選項 b ) decision（決定）最符合文意。

# 4 - 1. ～ 4 - 2.

**聽力原文：**

An unexpected windstorm hit the south Puget Sound region early yesterday morning, knocking down power lines and causing blackouts in many parts of Greater King County. Winds of up to 40 miles per hour sent tree limbs flying into storefront windows throughout downtown Seattle, forcing many small business owners to close down as early as 11:00 a.m.

Possibly most upsetting was the extremely low voter turnout for the City Council elections brought about by the hazardous weather conditions. City officials are debating whether to allow late absentee ballots due to the unprecedented election day storm.

**原文翻譯：**

昨日清晨一場意外的風暴襲擊了普吉灣南方，損壞許多電線並造成 Greater King 縣多處停電。高達每小時 40 哩的風速，使得樹枝飛進西雅圖市中心的商店櫥窗，迫使許多小商店在早上 11 點就打烊。

或許最令人沮喪的是，因為惡劣的天候造成市議會選舉極低的投票率。市府官員仍在辯論是否能因為這場空前的風暴而接受缺席者遲來的選票。

# 4 - 1.

**答案：** c ) A windstorm（風暴）

**中譯：** 普吉灣南方發生了什麼事？

　　a ) 反政府遊行　　　　　　　　b ) 洪水

　　c ) 風暴　　　　　　　　　　　d ) 商店搶案

**題解：** 第一句就很清楚點出 An unexpected windstorm hit the south Puget Sound... 所以是
選項 c ) A windstorm（風暴）。

# 4 - 2.

**答案：** b ) Early morning（清晨）

**中譯：** 問題是什麼時間發生的？

　　a ) 傍晚　　　　　　　　　　　b ) 清晨

　　c ) 中午　　　　　　　　　　　d ) 午夜

**題解：** 第一句就指出 ...early yesterday morning... 所以是選項 b ) Early morning（清晨）。

# 題解 3

## 1.

**答案**：a ) busy（忙碌的）

**中譯**：來電者若打進忙線中的分機，將會被轉入語音系統。

    a ) 忙碌的　　　　　b ) 可利用的　　　　c ) 可進入的　　　d ) 準備好的

**題解**：由句末的轉入語音系統可判斷出前面應是忙線的狀態，因此選項 a ) busy（忙碌的）最符合文意。

## 2.

**答案**：b ) hesitate（猶豫）

**中譯**：如果你對工作內容程序有任何問題，請別猶豫儘管跟人事部門聯絡。

    a ) 匆忙　　　　　b ) 猶豫　　　　　c ) 朝……行進　　d ) 催促

**題解**：人事部門可以解答對工作的疑惑，因此是鼓勵人們發問，只有選項 b ) hesitate（猶豫）最符合文意。

## 3.

**答案**：d ) phones（電話）

**中譯**：森林公園因為強烈的冬季風暴而吸引了媒體焦點和遊客，入園請攜帶衛星電話以便於緊急時可隨時報警。

a）碟型天線　　　　b）中心　　　　c）電視　　　　d）電話

題解：依據 connect you to 911（報警）可推論出旅客要帶的應是 d）phones（電話）。

# 4 - 1. ～ 4 - 2.

**聽力原文：**

You've reached the Preston Family Counseling Center. If you're a first-time caller or have any questions about us, please hold, and one of our operators will assist you momentarily. If you need to reschedule or cancel an appointment, press "2" now. If you would like to leave a message for your counselor or any of the staff, enter the three-digit code number of that person now. Office hours are between 10:00 a.m. and 9:00 p.m., Monday through Friday. Thank you for calling, and we hope we can be of assistance to you and your family.

**原文翻譯：**

這裡是 Preston Family 輔導中心。如果你是第一次打電話進來或有任何想問我們的問題，請稍候，我們的接線生將馬上為你服務。若你需要重新預約時間或取消預約，請按「2」。若你想留言給你的輔導員或其他人員，直接輸入該位人員的 3 位數分機號碼即可。辦公時間是週一到週五早上 10 點到晚上 9 點。感謝你的來電，我們希望能為你和你的家庭提供幫助。

# 4 - 1.

答案：c）Cancel an appointment.（取消預約。）

中譯：當人們在電話裡聽到上述留言可以做什麼？

　　　a）接受輔導。　　　　b）跟他們的家人通話。

　　　c）取消預約。　　　　d）購買治療書籍。

**題解**：文中提到 ...need to reschedule or cancel an appointment, press "2" ... 因此可得知可在電話裡改期或取消預約。

# 4 - 2. 🎧 ···························································································

**答案**：c) 10:00 a.m. to 9:00 p.m.（早上 10 點到晚上 9 點）

**中譯**：辦公室何時開放？

    a) 週一到週六                b) 全天 24 小時

    c) 早上 10 點到晚上 9 點        d) 一週七天

**題解**：文中最後提到 ...Office hours are between 10:00 a.m. and 9:00 p.m., 因此是選項 c ) 10:00 a.m. to 9:00 p.m.（早上 10 點到晚上 9 點）。

# 題解 4

## 1.

答案：b) remind（提醒）

中譯：既然夏天快到了，我們要提醒您如何使用房間的空調。

　　　a) 記得　　　　　　　b) 提醒　　　　　c) 挽回　　　　　d) 保持

題解：因為夏天來臨需要用到空調，所以選項 b) remind（提醒）最符合文意。

## 2.

答案：c) past due（過期的）

中譯：我們想提醒您的 1,998 歐元帳款已過期，若有任何特殊原因導致延遲付款，請來電告知我們。

　　　a) 過熟的　　　　　b) 不成熟的　　　c) 過期的　　　　d) 收支平衡

題解：由句末的 failing to remit the payment（未能如期付款）可推論出前面應填的是 c) past due（過期的）款項。

## 3.

答案：c) deadlines（截止日期）

中譯：WorkOrganizer 是一套強而有效的時間管理系統軟體，它可以幫您有效率地追蹤任務進度並提醒您截止日期。

a）死角　　　　　　b）僵局　　　　　　c）截止日期　　　　d）門栓

**題解**：因為是管理時間的軟體，所以答案必定與時間相關，只有選項 c）deadlines（截止日期）最符合要求。

# 4 - 1. ～ 4 - 2.

**聽力原文：**

Your attention, please. The Ponte Verde Beach Lifeguard Service will be closing down now. We ask all swimmers to come out of the water. We also advise all surfers to come out of the water as well. The darker conditions make it difficult to see. We would also like to ask all of you for your cooperation in keeping the beach clean, and remind all dog owners to pick up after their dogs. Lifeguard service will resume at 9:00 tomorrow morning. Thank you and good night.

**原文翻譯：**

請注意，Ponte Verde 海灘救生服務即將關閉。請所有游泳者離開水面。我們也建議所有衝浪者離開水面。黑暗使得能見度降低。我們希望您能配合維護海灘的清潔，並提醒所有狗主人要記得清理狗的排泄物。救生服務將在明早九點開始。感謝您並祝您有個愉快的夜晚。

# 4 - 1. 🎧

**答案**：c）At a public beach（在公共海灘）

**中譯**：這項廣播可能在哪裡發生？

a）在游泳池　　　　　　　　　　b）在飯店

c）在公共海灘　　　　　　　　　d）在港口

題解：從 Beach Lifeguard Service（海灘救生服務）和 swimmers（游泳者）和 surfers（衝浪者）等字可以判斷出該處是 c) At a public beach（在公共海灘）。

# 4 - 2.

答案：a) At sunset（日落時）

中譯：這項廣播何時發生？

　　a) 日落時　　　　　　　　　　b) 午餐時間

　　c) 早上　　　　　　　　　　　d) 深夜

題解：從救生服務即將關閉到逐漸變黑的天候（The darker condition）可以判斷出應是在 a) At sunset（日落時）。

# 題解 5

## 1.

**答案**：d ) interview（面談）

**中譯**：在面談之前你可以利用一份核對清單來確認自己已準備妥當，並有相當自信能夠取得那份工作。

    a ) 開端          b ) 視察          c ) 審問          d ) 面談

**題解**：由 getting that job 得知是要求職，所以可以判斷 use a checklist 用核對清單是為了準備去面試，因而選擇 d ) interview（面談）是最適合的答案。

## 2.

**答案**：b ) consumption（消耗）

**中譯**：我們相當確信地球暖化與人口增長和石化燃料的消耗密切相關。

    a ) 例外          b ) 消耗          c ) 消費者          d ) 絕種

**題解**：由 global warming 推論是和 fossil fuel 的大量使用有關，因此選擇 b ) consumption（消耗）。

## 3.

**答案**：a）better（更佳）

**中譯**：分析師認為較為低價的新產品，會比其原有的產品賣得更好。

　　　a）更佳　　　　　　b）更糟　　　　　c）最多　　　　　d）最少

**題解**：由 positive 知道分析家給予正面評價，因此對於銷售當然選擇樂觀的 a）better（更佳）。

## 4 - 1. ～ 4 - 2.

**聽力原文：**

Hello and welcome to Total Health. My name is Dana. I'll be your fitness consultant today. First of all, I need to make sure that all of you have read and signed the health release form. You cannot use the facilities until this has been signed. Next, we'll get you started on your fitness files. You can use this to record all of your vital statistics like weight, blood pressure, etc. And, it can help you keep track of your workout regimen. Then, we'll get you acquainted with all of the machines in the weight room. If you have any questions, please feel free to ask me at any time.

**原文翻譯：**

您好並歡迎來到Total Health！我的名字叫做 Dana 。我將會是您今天的健身顧問。首先，我必須先確認你們全部都仔細閱讀過健康狀況表格，並已經在上面簽名。在還沒簽名前，各位將無法使用任何設施。接下來，我們會和你一同開始建立你的健身檔案。你可以用這個紀錄你所有重要的生理機能指數，像是體重、血壓等。此外，它能幫你記錄你的健康養生訓練。再來，我們會讓您熟識重訓室裡所有的器材。如果您有任何問題，可以隨時詢問我。

## 4 - 1. 🎧

答案：c) At a health club（在一家健身俱樂部）

中譯：這段話是在什麼地方說的？

a) 在露營區　　　　　　　　　b) 在一間醫院

c) 在一家健身俱樂部　　　　　d) 在學校

題解：由說話的地點是在 Total Health，以及說話者自我介紹為一名健身顧問 fitness consultant 得知說話地點為一家健身俱樂部。

## 4 - 2. 🎧

答案：c) A health form（健康表格）

中譯：什麼東西必須簽名？

a) 買賣合約　　　　　　　　　b) 一份簽到單

c) 健康表格　　　　　　　　　d) 一個資料夾

題解：由 ...signed the health release form 得知需要填寫的是一份健康表。

# 題解 6

## 1.

**答案**：c ) ensure（確保）

**中譯**：請在付款截止的五個工作天前寄出你的款項，以確保能及時送達。

　　a ) 包含　　　　　b ) 澄清　　　　　c ) 確保　　　　　d ) 保護

**題解**：為了要確保及時送達所以必須提前寄出，選項 c ) ensure 最符合文意。

## 2.

**答案**：c ) objects（物體）

**中譯**：為避免外來物進入生產線上的產品，必須戴上髮網。

　　a ) 訪客　　　　　b ) 政策　　　　　c ) 物體　　　　　d ) 目標

**題解**：髮網能夠圈住頭髮使其不掉落，因此能避免外來物體 ( 頭髮 ) 進入產品，選項 c ) 最符合文意。

## 3.

**答案**：b ) exposure（曝光率）

**中譯**：我們的公關團隊會將你投遞的文案刊在全歐洲主要的刊物上，以確保你的新產品在此地區能有最高的曝光率。

　　a ) 解釋　　　　　b ) 曝光率　　　　　c ) 出口　　　　　d ) 高興

**題解**：因為會刊登在全歐洲主要的刊物上，因此產品會有相當高的曝光率。

# 4 - 1. ～ 4 - 2.

**聽力原文：**

If you are planning a move to another city, state, or even if you're just moving across town. Big Western Movers is the company you can trust. We have over 50 years in the domestic and commercial moving business and have moved everything from a grand piano to a pet elephant. Big Western Movers has 18 trucks and has assisted people moving all over North America, including Alaska. Our professionally trained movers will ensure safe and reliable transport of all your household items.

So if you're moving, leave the worries to Big Western Movers. We can handle the job for you.

**原文翻譯：**

如果你計畫要搬到其他城市，或只是搬到另一個鎮，你可以信賴 Big Western 搬家公司。我們在家庭與商業搬運有 50 年的經驗，從大鋼琴到寵物象都搬過。Big Western 搬家公司有 18 台卡車，而且已經協助人們搬運到全北美包含阿拉斯加等地。我們專業的搬運工人會確保你的所有家當都能安全可靠的送達。

所以如果你要搬家，就交給 Big Western 搬家公司吧。我們可以幫你辦事。

# 4 - 1. 🎧

**答案**：b）A moving company（搬家公司）

**中譯**：以下何者是對這家公司的最佳描述？

a）旅行社　　　　　　　　　　　b）搬家公司

c）在阿拉斯加的公司　　　　　　d）卡車租賃公司

題解：從文意中的 domestic and commercial moving business（家庭與商業搬運）和 professionally trained movers（專業搬運工人）可判斷出該公司是 b）搬家公司。

# 4 - 2.

答案：d）Only North America（只有北美）

中譯：這家公司在哪裡提供服務？

a）只在美國西部　　　　　　　　b）北美和歐洲

c）全球　　　　　　　　　　　　d）只有北美

題解：文中提到 ...assisted people moving all over North America... 因此可得知服務範圍是 d）只有北美。

# 題解 7

## 1.

**答案**：d ) dress（服裝）

**中譯**：員工在代表公司出席銷售會議時應該要遵守服裝規定，穿著正式服裝。

a ) 別針　　　　b ) 道德的　　　　c ) 刑事的　　　　d ) 服裝

**題解**：從 wear formal attire（穿著正式服裝）可以判斷出空格應填 d ) dress（服裝）。

## 2.

**答案**：b ) replaced（取代）

**中譯**：Sato 先生應該要出席這場會議，但最後卻是陳女士取代他出席。

a ) 改變　　　　b ) 取代　　　　c ) 代替　　　　d ) 遷移

**題解**：由文意可得知陳女士替 Sato 先生出席了會議，因此選項 b ) replaced（取代）最符合文意。

## 3.

**答案**：a ) fine（罰款）

**中譯**：駕駛人不應把汽車停在黃線區，否則將會因違法行為而被罰款。

a）罰款　　　　b）注意　　　　c）費用　　　　d）稅

題解：從 illegal behavior（違法行為）可以判斷出空格應為 a）fine（罰款）。

# 4 - 1. ～ 4 - 2.

聽力原文：

Hello Frank, this is Stella. I'm sorry I couldn't talk to you personally. I got the tickets for the Saturday concert like you asked. The orchestra seats were all sold out, but the saleslady told me the loge seats were better for sound and that we could bring binoculars. She also said that we should arrive early to avoid the big crowds. I'm thinking we could have a meal in the parking lot before the show. I have a hibachi and a folding table. Call me back as soon as you get this message. Thanks, bye.

原文翻譯：

哈囉，Frank, 我是 Stella。很遺憾不能親口跟你說。我拿到你要的週六演唱會門票了。頭等席都賣完了，但售票員告訴我包廂座位的音效比較好，而且我們可以帶望遠鏡。她也說我們應該提早到場以避開人潮。我想我們可以在開演前先在停車場吃飯。我有一個烤肉爐和折疊桌。聽到留言請盡快回電。謝謝，再見。

# 4 - 1.

答案：c）Go to a concert（去一場演唱會）

中譯：Frank 和 Stella 這週末要做什麼？

　　　a）去一個烤肉派對　　　　b）去露營

　　　c）去一場演唱會　　　　d）去一個海灘派對

題解：文中第二句提到 ...Saturday concert（週六演唱會），因此可得知他們是要去 c）Go to a concert（去一場演唱會）。

## 4 - 2. 🎧 ..............................................................................................

**答案：** a ) From an answering machine（答錄機）

**中譯：** Frank 應該是從哪裡聽到 Stella 的留言？

    a ) 答錄機                        b ) 公眾廣播

    c ) 由朋友                           d ) 親自

**題解：** 從 ...couldn't talk to you personally（不能口跟你說）和 ...Call me back（回電給我），可以判斷出此留言是 a ) From an answering machine（答錄機）。

# 題解 8

## 1.

**答案**：c ) emergency exits（緊急出口）

**中譯**：為了您的安全，飛機上分別有四個緊急出口。

　　 a ) 乘客　　　　　 b ) 機組人員　　　　 c ) 緊急出口　　　 d ) 餐車

**題解**：因為牽涉到安全，因此選項 c ) emergency exits（緊急出口）最符合文意 c ) emergency exits（緊急出口）。

## 2.

**答案**：c ) overlooking（俯瞰）

**中譯**：White Cliffs 飯店座落在 350 呎高的崖頂，能夠俯瞰美麗的地中海。

　　 a ) 預定過多　　 b ) 過度擁擠　　　 c ) 俯瞰　　　　 d ) 淹沒

**題解**：從 atop （在頂端）可判斷出飯店的位置很高，因此選項 c ) overlooking（俯瞰）最符合文意。

## 3.

**答案**：b ) access（通路）

**中譯**：主教會議中心位在 Liverpool 市中心且交通便利，你無法找到比它更理想的集會地點了。

a）入口　　　　b）通路　　　　c）出口　　　　d）積聚

**題解**：從文中得知是指主教會議中心地點便利，因此選項 b）access（通路）最符合文意。

# 4 - 1. ～ 4 - 2.

**聽力原文：**

Registered nurses are urgently needed. Positions are available immediately for qualified registered nurses with at least one year of experience to fill long and short-term, long-distance or local assignments. The pay scale is up to 45 dollars an hour with excellent benefits. Many hospitals are in desperate need of qualified RNs and are offering sign-on bonuses in addition to great salaries. Our company works with 400 hospitals located throughout the U.S. with new hospitals being added daily. Choose the state where you want to work. Escape the snow and freezing temperatures and spend the winter employed at a hospital in sunny Florida, California or even Hawaii! You must be a U.S. citizen to apply.

**原文翻譯：**

急需有執照的護士。徵求有一年以上工作經驗、能夠勝任長短期、遠距或本地的派遣，具執照的合格護士。薪酬高達每小時 45 美元並有豐厚福利。許多醫院急需具執照的合格護士，除了優渥薪水外也提供簽約獎金。本公司與全美四百家醫院合作，新的合作對象與日俱增。選擇你想工作的州，逃離下雪和低溫，你可以在陽光充沛的佛羅里達、加州甚至是夏威夷的醫院工作來度過冬天。你必須是美國公民才能申請。

# 4 - 1.

**答案**：b）Experienced American nurses（有經驗的美國護士）
**中譯**：這個廣告是給誰看的？

a ) 有抱負的護士　　　　　　　b ) 有經驗的美國護士

c ) 想在海外工作的護士　　　　d ) 住在寒冷地方的護士

題 解 ： 從 ...at least one year of experience（至 少 一 年 經 驗 ）和 ...You must be a U.S.
citizen（必須是美國公民）可以判斷出廣告要徵的是 b ) Experienced American
nurses.（有經驗的美國護士）。

# 4 - 2.

答案 ： c ) In the state the nurse chooses（護士自己選的州）

中譯 ： 合格的護士會被分到哪裡？

a ) 佛羅里達、加州或夏威夷　　b ) 海外的某處

c ) 護士自己選的州　　　　　　d ) 最缺乏護士的地方

題 解 ： 文中提到 Choose the state where you want to work.（選擇你想工作的州） 因此可
得知護士可以自己選擇，選項 c ) In the state the nurse chooses（護士自己選的州）
最符合文意。

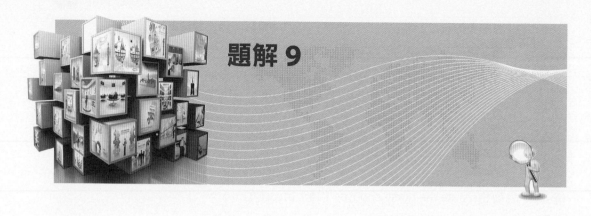

題解 9

## 1.

答案：c ) improvement（進步）

中譯：多數研究報告指出在職訓練方案有正面效果；參與訓練 30 天以上的員工，在表現上都有顯著的進步。

 a ) 暗示　　　　　b ) 印象　　　　　c ) 進步　　　　　d ) 惡化

題解：由題目中的 positive effects 得知，只有 c ) improvement（進步）符合題意。

## 2.

答案：b ) reported（舉發）

中譯：Kalihi 的居民舉發住家附近有人違法傾倒垃圾，抱怨情況有惡化趨勢，並造成潛在的健康威脅。

 a ) 回答　　　　　b ) 舉發　　　　　c ) 告訴　　　　　d ) 視為

題解：本題主詞為 residents，看似四個選項都可以接續其後；但 a ) answer 後面通常是接續 question, phone, door, letter 等字詞；c ) told 作「講述」解釋時，後面須有「事物」及「人」當受詞；d ) regard 不符合句意，只有 b ) reported 是正解。

# 3.

**答案：** d ) threatened（威脅）

**中譯：** 一位在東威靈頓街的便利商店店員告稱，他熟識的某人威脅他，並將在當晚搶劫商店。

a ) 安慰        b ) 勸告        c ) 推薦        d ) 威脅

**題解：** 由題目中的 ...said he would rob the store that night. 得知，只有 d ) threatened 符合句意。

# 4 - 1. ～ 4 - 2.

**聽力原文：**

And now for a news update. A mild earthquake measuring a magnitude of 4.7 was felt throughout the Los Angeles Basin. Minimal damage has been reported at La Loma, the earthquake's epicenter, and no injuries have been reported. The earthquake hit at 5:37 as commuters were making their way home. Small aftershocks are expected.

In other news, the governor will be holding a question-and-answer session with the media tomorrow at the governor's mansion. The state's current energy crisis will be the topic of the day as the governor attempts to tackle this ever-growing, statewide concern.

**原文翻譯：**

現在報導最新狀況：整個洛杉磯盆地都感覺到規模 4.7 的輕微地震。據報，在震央的 La Loma 地區有些微災情，但沒有人員受傷。地震發生在下午 5 點 37 分，正是通勤族下班返家的時間。預期會有些餘震發生。

其他新聞方面，州長將於明天在官邸舉行答詢式的記者會。本州目前的能源危機將是當天的主題，州長試圖要處理這項全州日益關心的議題。

# 4 - 1. 🎧

答案：b ) A small amount（一點點）

中譯：地震造成多少災害？

a ) 非常大　　　　　　　　　　　b ) 一點點

c ) 有些人受傷。　　　　　　　　d ) 有些建築倒塌。

題解：從文中的 Minimal damage, no injuries have been reported 得知，只有 b ) A small
amount 是正解。

# 4 - 2. 🎧

答案：b ) During the afternoon commute（在下午的返家時間）

中譯：地震何時發生？

a ) 一大早　　　　　　　　　　　b ) 在下午的返家時間

c ) 在上午的通勤時間　　　　　　d ) 中午時間

題解：從文中的 The earthquake hit at 5:37 as commuters were making their way home.
得知，只有 b ) During the afternoon commute 是正解。

# 題解 10

## 1.

答案：c ) feasibility（可行性）

中譯：研究人員獲得 2 萬英鎊，去分析在 Bourne 河上建築水壩的可行性。

a ) 彈性　　　　　b ) 移動性　　　　　c ) 可行性　　　　　d ) 一致

題解：從 analyze...of constructing a dam... 得知，只有 c ) feasibility（可行性）符合句意。

## 2.

答案：b ) contract（合約）

中譯：市政府將清理街道的合約授予一家清潔公司，因為越來越多的城市將這類服務對外招標，以取得價格競爭的優勢。

a ) 獎品　　　　　b ) 合約　　　　　c ) 獎金　　　　　d ) 獎章

題解：從題目中的 as more cities put services out to bid 得知，這是指對外招標的事宜，只有 b ) contract（合約）符合句意。

## 3.

答案：a ) host（主辦）

中譯：倫敦獲得主辦 2010 奧運會的權利，在最後一輪的投票中，以微小差距擊敗歐洲對手巴黎。

a）主辦　　　　　b）花費　　　　　c）招待　　　　　d）水管

**題解**：主辦各類活動的動詞是 host，因此得知 a）host（主辦）是正解。

# 4 - 1. ~ 4 - 2.

**聽力原文：**

We are very happy to announce that this year's annual employee awards banquet will be held in the grand ballroom of the elegant Adams Hotel. If you have not yet received your tickets, please call the personnel office immediately. We hope you'll join the president and board of directors in honoring this year's award winners.

**原文翻譯：**

我很高興向各位宣布，本年度員工頒獎晚會將在高雅的 Adams 飯店的宴會廳舉行。如果你還未收到入場券，請立刻打電話到人事室。希望大家都能和總裁以及董事會一起來表揚本年度的得獎者。

# 4 - 1. 🎧

**答案**：b）To honor workers（表揚員工）

**中譯**：此活動的目的為何？

a）慶祝一項新的合併案　　　　b）表揚員工

c）計畫下年度的策略　　　　　d）宣布利潤

**題解**：從文中 ...this year's annual employee awards banquet will be held... 得知，因此 b）To honor workers（表揚員工）為正解。

# 4 - 2.

答案： d ) Telephone the personnel office.（打電話給人事室。）

中譯： 如何能拿到晚會入場券？

　　　a ) 到飯店領取。　　　　　　　　b ) 打電話給總裁。

　　　c ) 聯絡董事會。　　　　　　　　d ) 打電話給人事室。

題 解： 從文中 If you have not yet received your tickets, please call the personnel office immediately. 得知，因此 d ) Telephone the personnel office.（打電話給人事室。）為正解。

# Persons
# 人際溝通

# 題解 1

## 1.

**答案**：d ) benefits（利益）

**中譯**：NIL 董事會最後同意和工會協調，為解雇員工提供更好的福利。

　　a ) 罰款　　　　　　　b ) 規則　　　　　　c ) 優點　　　　　　d ) 利益

**題解**：從董事會 Board of Directors 和工會 the unions 可以了解兩個對立關係的組織相互協商是要為爭取員工更好的 d ) benefits（利益）。

## 2.

**答案**：a ) targets（目標）

**中譯**：設定減少二氧化碳目標有助於與居民溝通，並促使他們及時達到減量需求。

　　a ) 目標　　　　　　　b ) 策略　　　　　　c ) 情形　　　　　　d ) 方案

**題解**：從 setting 以及減少二氧化碳 carbon dioxide reduction 可推論是要設定目標，所以 a ) targets（目標）最符合文意。

## 3.

**答案**：c ) landlord（房東）

**中譯**：如果你不能和房東協議降房租，至少可以詢問是否能延遲付款。

　　a ) 房客　　　　　　　b ) 地標　　　　　　c ) 房東　　　　　　d ) 批發商

**題解**：從 rent（房租）和 delay payment（延遲付款）可得知要協議 negotiate 的對方應是 c）landlord（房東）。

# 4 - 1. ～ 4 - 2.

**聽力原文：**

Information Technology Services is a world-class developer of Internet-based medical information management tools. The company's main product, Healthmaster, delivers up-to-the-minute medical data to healthcare organizations, helping clinicians make faster healthcare decisions. A physician deciding how to treat a certain illness, for example, can quickly view an online database of current treatments as well as communicate with other physicians and experts on the subject before making crucial decisions. The software gives more useful information in less time than any other product on the market, and it does so at a very affordable price.

**原文翻譯：**

Information Technology Services 是網路醫療資訊管理系統的頂尖研發者。該公司的主力產品 Healthmaster 為醫療機構提供最即時的醫療資訊，幫助臨床醫生更快速地做出醫療處置。舉例來說，當醫師針對特定病例做醫療決定前，可以快速瀏覽現今最新醫療處置的線上資料庫，也可以和其它的醫師與專家討論。這套軟體提供了比市場上任何商品更快速而有用的資訊，並且價格合理。

# 4 - 1.

**答案**：a）The Internet（網路）
**中譯**：Healthmaster 是以什麼作為媒介？

a）網路　　　　　　　　　b）技術手冊
c）新電腦硬體　　　　　　d）語音訊息

題解： 文章第一句 ...developer of Internet-based medical information... 指出該公司的服務是以網路為主，因此可知其主力產品 Healthmaster 是以 a ) The Internet（網路）作為媒介。

## 4 - 2. 🎧 ...................................................................................................................................

答案： b ) Manage medical information.（管理醫療資訊）

中譯： 這套軟體的用途是？

a ) 提供醫療訓練                b ) 管理醫療資訊

c ) 宣布重要發現                d ) 執行醫療行為

題解： 從文章中提到軟體……網路醫療資訊管理系統 Internet-based medical information management tools...delivers up-to-the-minute medical data...gives more useful information... 因此可得知該軟體是用來 b ) Manage medical information.（管理醫療資訊）。

# 題解 2

## 1.

**答案**：b ) documents（文件）

**中譯**：我在前往會議地點的途中，突然想到自己忘記帶會議文件。

　　a ) 食譜　　　　　　b ) 文件　　　　　　c ) 劑量　　　　　　d ) 船塢設備

**題解**：關鍵字在 meeting（會議），因此只有選項 b ) documents（文件）最符合文意。

## 2.

**答案**：c ) predicting（預料）

**中譯**：在這種情況下，公司未來會發生什麼事情是無法預料。

　　a ) 取得　　　　　　b ) 呈現　　　　　　c ) 預料　　　　　　d ) 提議

**題解**：由句末 in the future（未來）可推論出未來是無法預料的，因此 c ) predicting（預料）。

## 3.

**答案**：b ) occurred（出現）

**中譯**：我們從未想到這項計畫會對第二季的獲利造成如此顯著的提升。

　　a ) 發生　　　　　　b ) 出現

　　c ) 孵化　　　　　　d ) 遮掩

# 4 - 1. ～ 4 - 2.

**聽力原文：**

Tonight's program is a look back to the 20th century and two of the artists who significantly shaped its culture. Derek Heinz created socially conscious art in Europe between two cataclysmic wars and mirrored the aspirations of audiences in the United States in the 1930s and 1940s. Although there is a Heinz revival in progress, some of his greatest works for the German stage are still largely unheard today. Similarly, France's Pierre Martin, whose symphonies and other works used to figure prominently in concert programs, has experienced a decline in performances in recent years. Yet, both Heinz and Martin wrote decidedly modern works which spoke directly to millions of listeners.

**原文翻譯：**

今晚的節目要來回顧對 20 世紀文化影響深遠的兩位藝術家。Derek Heinz 在歐洲兩次劇烈的戰役中創造出具有社會意識的藝術，並反映出 1930 年代到 1940 年代間美國民眾的渴望。雖然目前 Heinz 的作品再度流行，但他一些以德國戲劇為主的大作，至今仍鮮為人知。 同樣地，法國的 Pierre Martin， 其交響樂和其他作品在音樂會中佔有重要地位，近年來也日漸式微。無論如何，Heinz 和 Martin 都寫出了決定性的現代作品，直接傳達給數以百萬的聽眾。

# 4 - 1. 🎧 ......

**答案**：c ) In Europe（在歐洲）

中譯：Derek Heinz 在哪裡創作？

　　　a ) 在美國　　　　　　　　　　b ) 在德國

　　　c ) 在歐洲　　　　　　　　　　d ) 在法國

題解：在文章第二句就提到 ...created socially conscious art in Europe（在歐洲創造出有社
　　　會意識的藝術）... 因此可得知答案是 c ) In Europe（在歐洲）。

## 4 - 2.

答案：b ) It is being performed less frequently.（比較少被演出。）

中譯：Martin 的作品近年來發生什麼事？

　　　a ) 又再度流行。　　　　　　　b ) 比較少被演出。

　　　c ) 和其他的作品混淆了。　　　　d ) 被現代藝術家更新。

題解：在文章第二段有提到 ...has experienced a decline in performance in recent years（近
　　　年來日漸式微）因此可得知他的作品在近年來 b ) 比較少被演出。

# 題解 3

## 1.

**答案**：b ) acknowledge（感謝）

**中譯**：感謝所有 Edinboro 的員工和眾多支持者的貢獻，讓公司得以鴻圖大展。

　　　　a ) 介紹　　　　　b ) 感謝　　　　　c ) 強調　　　　　d ) 答應

**題解**：從 ...the contributions of our staff and many supporters 員工和支持者的貢獻前面的 It is a pleasure（這是一份榮幸）可推論出應是致謝辭，可以了解發言者是要向大家致謝，因此選項 b ) acknowledge（感謝）最符合文意。

## 2.

**答案**：d ) pity（遺憾）

**中譯**：很遺憾他未能於在世時目睹自己的作品出版。

　　　　a ) 樂趣　　　　　b ) 優先　　　　　c ) 宴會　　　　　d ) 遺憾

**題解**：從 ...did not live to see...（不能活到……）可得知這是件遺憾的事，所以選項 d ) pity（遺憾）最符合文意。

## 3.

**答案**：b ) deception（欺騙）

**中譯**：令人惋惜的是，以榮譽為使命的機構寧以犧牲大眾利益的欺騙手法來保護自己的聲譽。

a）決定　　　　b）欺騙　　　　c）奚落　　　　d）推論

**題解**：從 shame 和 founded on honor 可推論出空格應是負面意味的字詞。為保護聲譽 protect their reputation 不惜欺騙大眾，因此 b）deception（欺騙）才符合文意。

# 4 - 1. ~ 4 - 2.

**聽力原文：**

Drawing a picture fully of St. Mary's Hospital in the time allotted permits reference to only a few of the interesting experiences and commendable advancements made during the period between 1979 and 1999. In that period, it was my privilege and pleasure to play a small part in the service to the suffering peoples of the world as the leader of this great institution whose 75th anniversary we recognize at this celebration. Every worth-while accomplishment traces back to some individual or group who was inspired by the ideal of humanity and willing to make the necessary sacrifices. St. Mary's Hospital could never have been a reality had it not been for the vision and determination of the Venerable Mother Helen Park of Boston, founder of the Sisters of the Poor of St. Mary on October 3, 1904, 96 years ago. The story of her life is perhaps the very definition of service through sacrifice.

**原文翻譯：**

在有限的時間裡，很難完整地介紹聖瑪麗醫院，請容我只能提到 1979 年到 1999 年間一些有趣的經驗和令人讚許的進展。在那段時間，我很榮幸能為受苦的世人略盡棉薄之力，擔任這個偉大機構的主管，如今我們一同歡慶 75 週年的到來。每項重要的成就都要歸功於一些受偉大人性啟發並願意做出必要犧牲的個人或團體。波士頓的 Helen Park 聖修女在 96 年前，1904 年十月三日創立了聖瑪麗安貧修女會。若不是她有相當的遠見和決心，聖瑪麗醫院絕不可能成立。她的生平事蹟或許是犧牲奉獻的最佳寫照。

## 4 - 1. 🎧

答案：c ) The former president of the hospital（醫院的前任院長）

中譯：說話者是誰？

    a ) 聖瑪麗                              b ) Helen Park

    c ) 醫院的前任院長                       d ) 安貧修女會的創立者

題解：從文中所提到的 ...to play a small part ...as the leader of this great institutionit was my privilege...as the leader... 因此可得知說話者是 c ) The former president of the hospital.（醫院的前任院長）。

## 4 - 2. 🎧

答案：b ) 75 years（75 年）

中譯：醫院已經成立多久了？

    a ) 96 年          b ) 75 年          c ) 20 年          d ) 10 年

題解：從文中所提到的 ...this great institution whose 75th anniversary we recognize at this celebration... 因此可得知醫院已成立 b ) 75 years（75 年）。

## 4 - 3. 🎧

答案：a ) Self-sacrificing groups or individuals（自我犧牲奉獻的團體或個人）

中譯：所有重要的成就源自於何處？

    a ) 自我犧牲奉獻的團體或個人              b ) 受苦的人們

    c ) 20 年                              d ) 10 年

題解：文中提到，每項重要的成就都要歸功於一些受偉大人性啟發並願意做出必要犧牲的個人或團體，因此選項 a ) Self-sacrificing groups or individuals（自我犧牲奉獻的團體或個人）最符合文意。

# 題解 4

## 1.

**答案**：b ) apologize（抱歉）

**中譯**：我們對於在備援磁碟從受損狀態修復期間所發生的伺服器斷電致上歉意。

　　　　a ) 表達　　　　　　b ) 抱歉　　　　　　c ) 感謝　　　　　　d ) 分析

**題解**：因為伺服器斷電造成了不便，因此選項 b ) 抱歉，最符合文意。

## 2.

**答案**：c ) road construction noise（路面施工的噪音）

**中譯**：因上週路面施工的噪音造成您在本飯店內不能好好休息，我們向您致上歉意。

　　　　a ) 貼心的服務　　　b ) 便宜的價格　　　c ) 路面施工的噪音　d ) 退費保證

**題解**：因為是道歉，所以可推論後面接的應是負面的選項，只有選項 c ) 路面施工的噪音最符合文意。

## 3.

**答案**：a ) unauthorized（未授權的）

**中譯**：街頭藝術家 Joseph Donelly 在聲明書中，為了他在未經授權處展示藝術作品而向市民道歉。

　　　　a ) 未授權的　　　　b ) 合法的　　　　c ) 統一的　　　　d ) 不重要的

題解：因為是道歉，因此負面的選項 a）未經授權，最符合文意。

# 4 - 1. ～ 4 - 2.

聽力原文：

Attention, shoppers. D.B. Mathews will be closing in 20 minutes. Please bring the apparel you wish to purchase to the nearest register. Registers are located on every floor. We accept cash, checks, all major credit cards and, of course, the D.B. Mathews charge card. We will be open tomorrow from 10:00 a.m. until 8:00 p.m. as usual, but we will be closed the day after tomorrow, on Monday, in order to take our inventory. We apologize for any inconvenience. Thank you for shopping at D.B. Mathews, and we hope to see you again soon.

原文翻譯：

顧客們請注意，D.B. Mathews 將在 20 分鐘後打烊。請將您想要購買的服飾拿到最近的櫃檯結帳。每層樓都有結帳櫃檯。我們接受現金、支票、所有主要的信用卡，當然，也接受 D.B. Mathews 簽帳卡。我們明天的營業時間一如往常是從早上 10 點到晚上 8 點，但後天，也就是星期一，因為要盤點存貨因此將不營業。造成任何不便我們深感歉意。感謝您光臨 D.B. Mathews，也期待很快能再次為您服務。

# 4 - 1. 🎧

答案：d）A clothing store（服飾店）

中譯：D.B. Mathews 是什麼公司？

　　　a）雜貨店　　　　　　　　　　b）大賣場

　　　c）信用卡公司　　　　　　　　d）服飾店

題解：從 ...bring the apparel you wish to purchase...（您希望購買的服飾）可得知這是一家 d）服飾店。

# 4 - 2.

答案：b）At the regular time（固定的時間）

中譯：D.B. Mathews 明天何時營業？

　　a）會關門　　　　　　　　　　b）固定的時間

　　c）早上 9 點到下午 5 點　　　　d）只有早上

題解：文中提到 ...open tomorrow from 10:00 a.m. until 8:00 p.m. as usual 因此可得知明天的營業時間是 b）固定的時間。

# 題解 5

## 1.

**答案**：c ) cancelled（取消）

**中譯**：已經離開這家健身中心的一些會員對該機構提出抱怨，因為在會員資格取消後該機構仍舊寄送帳單來。

a ) 更新　　　　　　b ) 回復　　　　　　c ) 取消　　　　　　d ) 安撫

**題解**：由題意得知，會員抱怨的理由必然是在其資格取消後仍舊收到帳單，因此只有 c ) cancelled（取消）是正解。

## 2.

**答案**：a ) illegally（非法地）

**中譯**：CleanGround 公司對 FDC 公司提出告訴，宣稱該公司違法將垃圾清運的服務併入街道清理的合約中。

a ) 非法地　　　　b ) 合法地　　　　c ) 寬大地　　　　d ) 經文選

**題解**：會對他人提出訴訟，必然是宣稱對方有違法事項，因此只有 a ) illegally（非法地）是正解。

## 3.

**答案**：d）employer（雇主）

**中譯**：如果你因為拒絕從事危險工作，為自身權益挺身而出，而遭受騷擾或被開除，可以對你的雇主提出訴怨。

a）雇員　　　　b）同事　　　　c）炮台　　　　d）雇主

**題解**：從題意中得知，因拒絕從事危險工作而受到騷擾或被開除，能對此提出訴願的對象自然是雇主，因此 d）employer（雇主）是正解。

## 4 - 1. ～ 4 - 2.

**聽力原文：**

Bering Aviation has come under fire recently with serious complaints from its union and much of society at large due to a rumor that corporate executives are thinking about a major move in manufacturing from its home base in western Washington to Mexico. After the economic treaties of NAFTA and GATT, every major aeronautical manufacturer in the U.S. has quietly shut down plants in the States and moved them to Mexico except for Bering.

Most recent was the closure of three plants of a competitor in California, later reestablished in northwest Mexico. Now it seems that such economic pressures are turning the attention of Bering's decision makers southward as well.

**原文翻譯：**

由於謠傳 Bering 航空製造公司的高階主管們，正考慮將其主要生產業務，從西華盛頓的總部移轉到墨西哥，因此受到來自工會及社會絕大多數人的強烈抨擊。在北美自由貿易協定及關稅貿易總協定的經濟協商後，除了 Bering 之外，所有美國主要的航空儀器製造商

都已經悄悄地關閉在美國的工廠，並遷往墨西哥。最近則是加州一間競爭對手的三座廠房關閉後，之後又在墨西哥西北部重新設立。目前這種經濟壓力，似乎引發 Bering 的關注，決策階層也傾向南移。

## 4 - 1. 🎧

**答案**：c) The rumor of the company's move（公司遷廠的謠言）

**中譯**：什麼事激怒了 Bering 航空的工會？

　　a) 公司主管的決定　　　　　　　b) 股東會

　　c) 公司遷廠的謠言　　　　　　　d) 經濟壓力

**題解**：從文中的 ...serious complaints from its union.... due to a rumor that corporate executives are thinking about a major move in manufacturing from its home base... 得知，故解答為 c) The rumor of the company's move.

## 4 - 2. 🎧

**答案**：d) It is still in the United States.（它還在美國。）

**中譯**：為何 Bering 航空是個例外？

　　a) 它已關閉廠房了。　　　　　　b) 它遭受了嚴重的抱怨與抨擊。

　　c) 它仍然是個航空儀器製造商。　　d) 它還在美國。

**題解**：從文中的 ...every major aeronautical manufacturer in the U.S. has quietly shut down plants... and moved them to Mexico except for Bering. 得知解答為 d) It is still in the United States.

# 題解 6

## 1.

**答案**：b ) privately（私下地）

**中譯**：報告指出 Ambrook 基金藉由私下表達政策意見，而非對大眾公開宣布，表現得宜。

    a ) 先前地　　　　b ) 私下地　　　　c ) 有生產力地　　　　d ) 有名望地

**題解**：從句末的公開宣布 announcing to the public 可推論出前面的反詞應是 b ) 私下地。

## 2.

**答案**：a ) Readers'（讀者的）

**中譯**：讀者的消費習慣通常會受口耳相傳而非書評所影響。

    a ) 讀者的　　　　b ) 作者的　　　　c ) 表演者的　　　　d ) 出版商的

**題解**：從句首的 buying habits（消費習慣）可推論出 a ) 讀者 最符合買書的文意。

## 3.

**答案**：b ) tolerance（容忍限度）

**中譯**：我們應瞭解誤差是無可避免的，並著重在誤差的容忍限度上，而非一味試著避免誤差。

    a ) 解脫　　　　b ) 容忍限度　　　　c ) 豁免　　　　d ) 豐富繁茂

**題解**：從前後文意可推論出誤差無法避免，所以 b ) 容忍限度，最符合文意。

## 4.

**聽力原文：**

What do you say we go to a ball game on Friday?

a ) I was busy.

b ) I hope he has fun.

c ) I would rather go to a movie.

**原文翻譯：**

我們星期五去看球賽好不好？

a ) 我很忙。

b ) 我希望他玩得開心。

c ) 我寧願去看電影。

**答案：** c ) I would rather go to a movie.（我寧願去看電影。）

**題解：** 問句問的是遊樂休閒，只有 c ) 看電影最符合邏輯。

## 5.

**聽力原文：**

W : Would you like some of my chicken?

M : I don't eat meat.

W : Oh, I'm sorry. How about some of this pasta?

**原文翻譯：**

女：你想吃一些雞肉嗎？

男：我不吃肉。

女：噢，我很抱歉。那來些義大利麵好嗎？

**答案：** d ) He is vegetarian.（他是素食者。）

**題解：** 從男士的回答 I don't eat meat.（我不吃肉。）可推論出 d ) 他是素食者。

# 題解 7

## 1.

**答案**：c ) outsourcing（外包）

**中譯**：許多公司寧可將勞力外包，也不願雇用臨時性或專案性的員工。

    a ) 獵取             b ) 會計             c ) 外包             d ) 資源

**題解**：從題目中得知，可以替代 hire temporary or project-based employees 的選擇，應該是勞力外包，故選 c ) outsourcing（外包）。

## 2.

**答案**：c ) issue（問題）

**中譯**：一項調查發現大多數的美國父母寧可待在家中教養小孩，也不願外出工作，如果收入不成問題。

    a ) 興趣             b ) 干擾             c ) 問題             d ) 保證

**題解**：從題目中得知，能夠待在家裡陪孩子、不工作，自然是因為收入不成問題，故選 c ) issue（問題）。

## 3.

**答案**：a ) convenience（便利性）

a ) 便利性　　　　　b ) 習俗　　　　　c ) 規避　　　　　d ) 通風

**題解**：選擇藥局的考量因素，除題目提供的 location，符合題意只有 a ) convenience（便利性）。

## 4. 🎧

**聽力原文：**

Would you like some coffee?

a ) I'd rather drink water.

b ) This coffee isn't hot.

c ) I like the smell of coffee.

**原文翻譯：**

來杯咖啡吧？

a ) 我寧可喝水。

b ) 這杯咖啡不熱。

c ) 我喜歡咖啡的味道。

**答案**：a ) I'd rather drink water.（我寧可喝水。）

**題解**：對方詢問是否要咖啡，只有 a ) I'd rather drink water.（我寧可喝水。），符合題意。

## 5. 🎧

**聽力原文：**

W : What kind of car do you drive to work?

M : Actually, I ride my bike to work for exercise.

W : So that's how you keep in such good shape.

**原文翻譯：**

女：你開哪種車上班？

男：實際上，我是騎腳踏車去上班當做運動。

女：所以這就是你維持好身材的方法。

**答案：** c）He prefers to exercise.（他喜歡運動。）

**中譯：** 為什麼男士不開車去上班？

　　　a）因為車子汙染空氣。　　　　　b）他喜歡騎摩托車。

　　　c）他喜歡運動。　　　　　　　　d）他的朋友叫他別開車。

**題解：** 由題中 I ride my bike to work for exercise. 得知答案為 c）He prefers to exercise.（他喜歡運動。）。

# 題解 8

## 1.

**答案**：a ) committee（委員會）

**中譯**：所有諮詢委員會的成員已經核准科技贊助費的提案。

 a ) 委員會　　　　 b ) 商品　　　　 c ) 佣金　　　　 d ) 海軍准將

**題解**：提案必須由人同意通過方能生效，因此只有選項 a ) committee（委員會）較符合文意。

## 2.

**答案**：c ) process（過程）

**中譯**：選民可能會訝異，他們去年冬天表決同意的大眾運輸方案，至今仍在州議會等待同意通過的階段。

 a ) 精確　　　　 b ) 預防　　　　 c ) 過程　　　　 d ) 起訴

**題解**：從 ...they approved last winter is still going through...（從去年冬天持續到現在）可得知這是一項漫長的過程，因此選項 c ) process（過程）最符合文意。

## 3.

**答案**：d ) board（董事會）

中譯：董事會會議可能會同意公司進軍速食業的主意。

　　a）舞廳　　　　　b）船　　　　　　c）老闆　　　　　d）董事會

題解：公司要擴展事業版圖需獲得組織的同意，因此選項d）board（董事會）較符合文意。

# 4 - 1. ～ 4 - 2.

**聽力原文：**

Epiphyte Incorporated is accepting applications for various positions in any of its three Pierce County locations. From programming to sales, a multitude of opportunities await creative, individualistic thinkers who work well in team situations and have a college degree.

Not yet a master programmer? Or maybe a freelance hacker who wants to settle down and start making your skills pay off? Epiphyte is interested in all college graduate applicants who think they can contribute to a friendly, imagination-supportive software company. Learn and grow as you work! Fax resumes to 253-544-7656 or e-mail to apply@epiphyte.com.

**原文翻譯：**

Epiphyte 企業正為旗下 Pierce 縣三個分部的各項職缺徵才。從程式設計到業務行銷，許多機會正等者有大學學歷者且富創意、團隊合作狀況良好的獨立思考者。你還不是職業程式設計者嗎？或你是自由業的網路駭客，但想要穩定下來發揮所長？ Epiphyte 歡迎所有自認可以對友善且鼓勵創意的軟體公司有所貢獻的大學畢業生。在工作中學習成長！傳真履歷至 253-544-7656 或傳電子郵件到 apply@epiphyte.com。

## 4 - 1. 🎧 ·····

**答案**：a ) Software（軟體）

**中譯**：Epiphyte 公司是做什麼樣的產品？

    a ) 軟體                    b ) 電腦

    c ) 錄音機               d ) 傳真機

**題解**：文末有提到該公司是 software company（軟體公司），因此可得知其產品是 a ) Software（軟體）最符合文意。

## 4 - 2. 🎧 ·····

**答案**：c ) None whatsoever（完全不需要）

**中譯**：需要有工作經驗才能申請嗎？

    a ) 要一點工作經驗          b ) 電腦的相關經驗

    c ) 完全不需要             d ) 研究的經驗

**題解**：文中提到的條件要求完全沒提到需要工作經驗，因此選項 c ) None whatsoever（完全不需要）最符合文意。

題解 9

## 1.

**答案**：b ) burns（燙傷）

**中譯**：若你必須把手提電腦放在大腿上，皮膚科醫師建議必須在其底下放隔熱板以避免被燙傷。

a ) 墜落　　　　b ) 燙傷　　　　c ) 割傷　　　　d ) 疤痕

**題解**：從 heat shield（隔熱板）可推論出要避免的風險是 b ) burns（燙傷）。

## 2.

**答案**：b ) recommended（建議）

**中譯**：要喝所有罐裝汽水前，強烈建議把罐子上方徹底清洗乾淨。

a ) 辨識　　　　b ) 建議　　　　c ) 競爭　　　　d ) 酬謝

**題解**：由文意可判斷喝汽水前清洗罐子是一項建議，因此選項 b ) recommended（建議）最符合要求。

## 3.

**答案**：a ) weight-loss（減重）

**中譯**：有些研究建議以長期來看，若你可以選擇少吃或多運動，運動會是減重較好的選擇。

**題解**：從邏輯判斷少吃和多運動都是減輕體重的方法，因此選項 a）weight-loss（減重）
最符合文意。

# 4 - 1. ～ 4 - 2.

**聽力原文：**

Those of you on your morning commute need to be aware that a one mile
section of 101 North has been closed. It seems that a truck carrying swimming
pool chemicals has overturned about 15 minutes ago. Police are directing traffic
away from the scene, just south of Vintage Oaks Shopping Center in Paloma. At
this time, we don't know what caused the accident, but it looks as if it will take
some time to clean up. If that is your normal commute route, we suggest you
take Jefferson Parkway north to 3rd Street before trying to get back on. Most
other traffic is being rerouted to State Highway 37. There was also a minor fender
bender just east of Rowan Avenue, but other than that, traffic is flowing along
nicely this morning.

And now we'll go over to Dave in the studio for the 8:00 a.m. weather report. Hi,
Dave.

**原文翻譯：**

在早晨通勤的人們需注意北向 101 號公路有一英里的路段已經封閉。約 15 分鐘前
一輛載泳池藥劑的卡車在此處翻覆。警察已在 Paloma 的 Vintage Oaks 購物中心
南方的事故現場指揮交通。目前我們無法得知意外起因，但似乎需要一段時間清
理現場。如果那是你的日常通勤路線，我們建議你在嘗試回到這條道路前，改走
北上的 Jefferson Parkway 到第三街。其他多數車輛都改道 37 號州道。在 Rowan
Avenue 東方也有一場輕微的車禍，但除此之外，今早的交通都還算順暢。

現在我們把現場交給 Dave，進行早上八點的氣象報告。哈囉，Dave。

# 4 - 1.

**答案：** b ) 8:00 a.m.（早上八點）

**中譯：** 這項資訊是何時廣播的？

a ) 早上 7:15                              b ) 早上 8:00

c ) 下午 1:01                              d ) 晚上 8:00

**題解：** 文末提到 ...for the 8:00 a.m. weather report...，因此可得知廣播時間是 b ) 8:00 a.m.（早上八點）。

# 4 - 2.

**答案：** a ) Not more than 15 minutes（不超過 15 分鐘）

**中譯：** 101 道路北方已經封閉多久了？

a ) 不超過 15 分鐘                         b ) 未明確指出

c ) 一整個早上                             d ) 一整天

**題解：** 文中提到路段封閉的情況是 ...truck carrying swimming pool chemicals has overturned about 15 minutes ago. 因此可得知從 15 分鐘前翻車就已經封閉路面，所以答案是 a ) Not more than 15 minutes（不超過 15 分鐘）。

# 題解 10

## 1.

**答案**：c ) eligible（合格的）

**中譯**：所有的全職員工都有資格加入五月一日開始執行的健康計畫。

　　a ) 易辨識的　　　　b ) 可食用的　　　　c ) 合格的　　　　d ) 能讀寫的

**題解**：從文意得知所有全職員工都能加入健康計畫，所以選項 c ) eligible（合格的）最符合文意。

## 2.

**答案**：b ) joining（加入）

**中譯**：從德國來的三位工程師將加入公司明年春季的大型計畫案。

　　a ) 出席　　　　　　b ) 加入　　　　　　c ) 享受　　　　　　d ) 參予

**題解**：從文意得知公司會延攬三位德籍工程師一起進行企劃案，所以選項 b ) joining（加入）最符合文意。

## 3.

**答案**：b ) available（可得的）

**中譯**：因為很多人想參加週六的頒獎典禮，因此將會提供大眾額外的公車運輸。

a）可連接的　　　b）可得的　　　c）額外的　　　d）可負擔的

**題解**：因觀禮人數眾多，需要更多的公車以紓解人潮，所以選項 b）available（可獲得的）最符合文意。

# 4 - 1. ～ 4 - 2.

**聽力原文：**

Remember what it was like to sit through a high school algebra or physics class and wonder how it related to real life? Well, learning has changed in Castle Rock. The Castle Rock Independent School District is now offering students an opportunity to apply what they learn in school to real-life work experiences. It's called School to Work. It's a pragmatic, community-driven approach to better prepare kids for college and careers by involving industry as training partners. School to Work is a positive project to improve education, help the economy and provide direction and support for the area's youth. If you want to learn more about School to Work opportunities and the schools and industries involved, please call 555-1815.That's 555-1815.

**原文翻譯：**

還記得高中時坐著上代數課或物理課並懷疑它們與現實生活的關聯嗎？在 Castle Rock 有不一樣的學習方式。Castle Rock 獨立校區現正提供學生將學校所學應用到真實工作經驗的機會。稱為「校外實習」。它採取務實的社會導向，藉由加入企業作為訓練合作對象，讓學生在未來大學學業和職涯上得到更好的準備。校外實習是一項積極改善教育的計畫，可幫助經濟發展並提供當地青年指導以及支持。如果你想得知更多校外實習的訊息、學校，及參與的產業，請打 555-1815 專線。專線是 555-1815。

## 4 - 1. 🎧

**答案**：d) Teach young people about work.（教導年輕人工作之事。）

**中譯**：這項計畫設計的目的為何？

    a) 為學校募款。               b) 讓成人獲得高中文憑。

    c) 教物理。                    d) 教導年輕人工作之事。

**題解**：文中提到該計畫目的是 ...better prepare kids for college and careers... 因此可得知答案是 d) Teach young people about work.（教導年輕人工作之事）。

## 4 - 2. 🎧

**答案**：b) Children are getting hands-on experience.

        （孩子可以獲得實際操作練習的經驗。）

**中譯**：Castle Rock 改變了什麼學習方式？

    a) 孩子不再被要求學習代數。    b) 孩子可以獲得實際操作練習的經驗。

    c) 孩子可以在家自習。          d) 當地商人會教課。

**題解**：由文中提到的 ...an opportunity to apply what they learn in school to real-life work experiences.（將學校所學應用到真實工作經驗的機會），因此可得知改變的學習方式是 b) Children are getting hands-on experience.（孩子可以獲得實際操作練習的經驗。）

# Objects
# or Events
# 事物說明

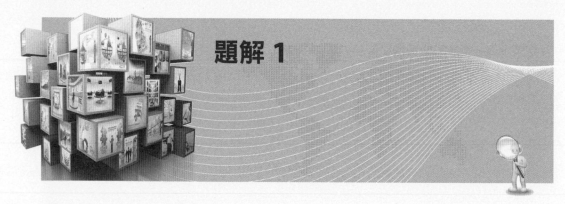

題解 1

## 1.

**答案**：a ) flooded（淹沒）

**中譯**：藉著下載我們的 CleanNet Filter 軟體，將可免於信箱被垃圾郵件淹沒。

a ) 淹沒　　　　b ) 茂盛　　　　c ) 起毛球　　　　d ) 漂浮

**題解**：從題意中得知，信箱只有被垃圾郵件「淹沒」的可能，其他選項都不符合文意，因此 a ) flooded（淹沒）為正解。

## 2.

**答案**：c ) calm（安靜）

**中譯**：為防止你的狗拉扯鍊條，在出門開始遛狗前，先等狗兒安靜下來。

a ) 跌倒　　　　b ) 過來　　　　c ) 安靜　　　　d ) 確定

**題解**：從題意中得知，防止狗拉扯鍊條，必然是先等牠安靜下來，才出門溜狗；因此 c ) calm（安靜）為正解。

## 3.

**答案**：a ) impulse（衝動）

**中譯**：藉著每個月對各支出項目設立特定的金額，可防止自己花錢在衝動性購買上。

a）衝動　　　　　b）挑釁　　　　c）準備　　　　d）即興作品

**題解**：從題意得知，每個月對支出設定金額上限，必然是為了防止「衝動性購買」，因此
a）impulse（衝動）為正解。

# 4 - 1. ～ 4 - 2.

**聽力原文：**

Tonight we're going to discuss sleep apnea, a disorder which causes sufferers to stop breathing repeatedly during their sleep, sometimes hundreds of times during the night and often for a minute or longer. Sleep apnea is an extremely common disorder, as common as adult diabetes. Yet still because of the lack of awareness by the public and healthcare professionals, the vast majority remain undiagnosed and therefore untreated. Risk factors include being male, overweight and over the age of 40, but sleep apnea can strike anyone at any age, even children.

Sleep apnea is caused by a blockage of the airway, usually when the soft tissue in the rear of the throat collapses and closes during sleep, or by the brain failing to signal the muscles to breathe, or by a combination of the two.

**原文翻譯：**

今晚我們要談論的是睡眠呼吸中止症，這類失調症狀會導致患者在睡覺時呼吸重複地中斷，有時候一整夜會有數百次，每次中斷時間長達一分鐘或更久。睡眠呼吸中止症是極為常見的症狀，如同成人糖尿病般普通。但由於大眾及健康護理專業人員對此缺乏認知，大多數患者未被診斷出，因此也未接受治療。罹患的危險因素包括男性、過重、及四十歲以上，但睡眠呼吸中止症可能侵襲各年齡層的人，甚至孩童。

睡眠中止症肇因於呼吸道阻塞，通常是由於睡覺時喉嚨後方的軟組織塌陷及閉合，或是大腦無法對掌管呼吸的肌肉發出訊息，也可能是兩者合併造成。

## 4 - 1.

答案：d ) Most people are unaware of it.（大多數的人對此毫無認知。）

中譯：為何大多數呼吸中止症的病例未接受治療？

a ) 它是非常罕見的疾病。　　　　b ) 無藥可醫。

c ) 它影響太多的人。　　　　　　d ) 大多數的人對此毫無認知。

題解：由文中的 Yet still because of the lack of awareness by the public and healthcare professionals, the vast majority remain undiagnosed and therefore untreated. 得知只有 d ) Most people are unaware of it.（大多數的人對此毫無認知。）為正解。

## 4 - 2.

答案：d ) Anyone（任何人）

中譯：哪些人可能會罹患此症？

a ) 男性　　　　　　　　　　　b ) 過重的人

c ) 老年人　　　　　　　　　　d ) 任何人

題解：由文中的 ...but sleep apnea can strike anyone at any age, even children 得知，只有 d ) Anyone（任何人）是正解。

# 題解 2

## 1.

**答案**：a ) alternative（替代選擇）

**中譯**：現今許多人會尋找較天然的替代品，來取代含糖和化學成分的碳酸飲料。

a ) 替代選擇　　　　b ) 資源　　　　c ) 觀點　　　　d ) 過程

**題解**：從句首的 instead of（替代），就可判斷是要取代不健康的碳酸飲料汽水，因此天
然的 a ) alternative 替代選擇，最符合文意。

## 2.

**答案**：d ) reduces（減少）

**中譯**：使用蔬菜油取代柴油，將可減少能引起溫室效應的氣體和微粒狀的污染物。

a ) 介紹　　　　b ) 誘惑　　　　c ) 推論　　　　d ) 減少

**題解**：蔬菜油比柴油所造成的污染少，因此可以得知答案是 d ) reduces（減少）。

## 3.

**答案**：a ) automatic（自動的）

**中譯**：大多賽車都是手排車而非自排的原因，在於手動的傳動裝置讓
駕駛更能掌控全車。

a ) 自動的　　　　　b ) 故意的　　　　　c ) 充滿活力的　　　d ) 電子的

**題解**：從空格前的 manual（手動的）可推論出與其相對的應是 a ) automatic（自動的）。

# 4. 🎧 ..........................................

**聽力原文**：

M1 : Has this week's supply of printer paper come yet?

M2 : No. The delivery truck now comes on Tuesday instead of Monday. It should be here this afternoon.

M1 : O.K. Can you call me when it gets here?

**原文翻譯**：

M1 : 這週的影印用紙送來了嗎？

M2 : 還沒。貨運車現在是星期二而不是星期一送貨。應該今天下午就會到了。

M1 : 好吧。如果貨到了麻煩你叫我一下好嗎？

**答案**：d ) The delivery schedule was changed.（運送日期改變了。）

**中譯**：為何影印紙還沒到貨？

a ) 公司紙用完了。　　　　　　　　b ) 卡車出了車禍。

c ) 公司星期四關門。　　　　　　　d ) 運送的行程改變了。

**題解**：從 M2 的回答中 ...now comes on Tuesday instead of Monday（改星期二而非星期一）因此可得知紙未到的原因是 d ) The delivery schedule was changed. 運送日期改變了。

# 題解 3

## 1.

**答案**：a) replaced（取代）

**中譯**：我對梨子和番茄過敏，如果可能的話，在裝運中我想用蘋果來取代。

    a) 取代          b) 讚美          c) 評論          d) 比較

**題解**：因為對梨子和番茄過敏，所以想用蘋果來取代。因此選項 a) replaced（取代）最符合文意。

## 2.

**答案**：c) supplement（補充）

**中譯**：請注意這本手冊只是為了提供資訊，並不能替代或補充產品的保證。

    a) 讚美          b) 評論          c) 補充          d) 執行

**題解**：從文意得知說明手冊並不能取代或補充產品保證，因此只有 c) supplement（補充）最符合 warranty（保證）。

## 3.

**答案**：d) defective（有缺陷的）

**中譯**：Takemi 先生很驚訝發現到半數的電腦零件都壞了必須更換。

    a) 偵探的          b) 傳染的          c) 保護的          d) 有缺陷的

題解：從句後的 replaced（更換）可推論出前面的空格應填 d）defective（有缺陷的）所以零件必須更換。

# 4 - 1. ～ 4 - 2.

聽力原文：

Good morning and thanks for joining Morning Workout here on Channel 5. Before we go into today's 20-minute aerobics routine, a little healthy eating advice. Listen to this: eat lots of bananas. Did you know that bananas are a good source of vitamin C and potassium? Bananas are low in fat, cholesterol and sodium. Bananas are also an excellent source of fiber that can lower the rate of cancer as well. And for athletes like you, bananas replace carbohydrates, glycogen and body fluids that you burn during exercise. Do you want to keep in shape? Exercise often and eat bananas! Ready for your workout? Let's go!

原文翻譯：

早安並感謝您收聽第五頻道的「晨間運動」。在進入今天例行的 20 分鐘有氧運動前，先提供一點健康飲食建議。聽聽以下這個：多吃香蕉。你知道香蕉是很好的維他命 C 和鉀的來源嗎？香蕉的脂肪、膽固醇和鈉含量都很低。香蕉同時也富含可以降低罹癌機率的纖維素。至於像你們這些運動的人，香蕉可以取代在運動中消耗的碳水化合物、醣類和體內水分。你想要維持窈窕身材嗎？多運動和吃香蕉！準備好要運動了嗎？我們開始吧！

# 4 - 1. 🎧

答案：c）They replace one's body fluids.（香蕉可以取代人體水分。）

中譯：為何運動員被推薦要吃香蕉？

a ) 香蕉讓人強壯。 　　　　　　　　b ) 香蕉能改善技巧。

c ) 香蕉可以取代人體水分。 　　　　b ) 香蕉可以增加速度。

題解：文章後段提到 ...bananas replace carbohydrates, glycogen and body fluids... 因此可
得知是 c ) 香蕉可以取代人體水分。

## 4 - 2.

答案：d ) Cancer（癌症）

中譯：哪種疾病是說話者宣稱香蕉可以降低罹患的機率？

a ) 心臟病 　　　　　　　　　　　b ) 感冒

c ) 糖尿病 　　　　　　　　　　　d ) 癌症

題解：文章中後段有提到 ...that can lower the rate of cancer... 因此可以得知是選項 d )
Cancer（癌症）。

# 題解 4

## 1.

**答案**：c ) alternative（替代方案）

**中譯**：科學家發現玩動態的電玩遊戲可以算是讓孩童適度運動的替代方案。

　　a ) 娛樂　　　　　　b ) 消費者　　　　　　c ) 替代方案　　　　d ) 交替

**題解**：從文意中可以得知，對孩童來說，玩電動也是種適度的運動，因此選項 c )
　　　　alternative（替代方案）最符合文意。

## 2.

**答案**：a ) regional（地區性）

**中譯**：農村外包可能也是委外的替代方案之一，此舉不但能節省費用也能協助發展地方經
　　　　濟。

　　a ) 地區性　　　　b ) 全球性　　　　c ) 廣大的　　　　d ) 寬廣的

**題解**：從農村外包 rural sourcing 又稱 rural outsourcing，是指美國部分公司開始轉
　　　　向與美國農村合作，取代過去越洋外包技術勞工。句中主體是農村外包，因
　　　　此只有選項 a ) regional（地區性）最適合文意。

## 3.

答案：b ) cost-effective（成本效益的）

中譯：對環城旅行來說，電動腳踏車是比汽車更加方便且經濟的替代品。

    a ) 消費的         b ) 成本效益的        c ) 加速的        d ) 免費的

題解：由文中可得知電動腳踏車比汽車有更多優點，因此選項 b ) cost-effective（成本效益的）最符合文意。

## 4 - 1. ～ 4 - 2.

聽力原文：

There are many natural alternatives to synthetic sweeteners for mild diabetics and the calorie-counting eater. From fruit-derived sweeteners to brown rice syrup, there are many ways to sweeten your coffee or even bake with. All contain their own distinct, rich flavor, have significantly less calories than traditional cane sugar, and if used in moderation affect the body less harshly than cane sugar. Synthetic sweeteners such as saccharin have dropped in popularity in recent years due to their containing unhealthy carcinogenic agents. Many former users of synthetic sweeteners have turned to natural methods, but have found that information is still hard to come by. For diabetics, before trying various natural sweeteners, it is wise to consult a doctor or naturopath to decide how they may affect your personal situation.

原文翻譯：

在對輕度糖尿病和計算熱量的飲食者來說，有很多天然替代品能取代人工甜味。從果糖到麥芽糖漿，有很多方式可以讓咖啡和烘培變甜。每一種都有其獨特的豐郁口感，熱量也比傳統蔗糖低，如果適

量攝取也較蔗糖不傷害人體。近年來人工甜劑像糖精因含有害的致癌物質已不再受歡迎。許多之前用人工甜劑的人已轉用天然的物質，但發現資訊仍然很難獲得。對糖尿病患來說，在嘗試任何天然甜劑之前，最好先諮詢醫生或自然療法治療師來決定自己的狀況是否適用。

## 4 - 1. 🎧

**答案**：d）Because they contain materials which are bad for your health
（因為它們含對健康有害的物質）

**中譯**：為何人工甜劑不再受歡迎？

a）因為它們很難吃 　　　　　　　b）因為它們很貴

c）因為它們落伍了 　　　　　　　d）因為它們含對健康有害的物質

**題解**：文章後段提到 ...due to their containing unhealthy carcinogenic agents... 因此可得知原因是選項 d）因為它們含對健康有害的物質。

## 4 - 2. 🎧

**答案**：a）Fruits and rice（水果和米）

**中譯**：取代人工甜劑的天然物質是由什麼東西提煉而成？

a）水果和米 　　　　　　　　b）糖精

c）蔗糖 　　　　　　　　　　d）黑糖漿

**題解**：文中提到 ...From fruit-derived sweeteners to brown rice syrup... 因此可得知是從 a）水果和米中提煉出來的。

# 題解 5

## 1.

**答案**：b ) insignificant（微不足道的）

**中譯**：一塊磚頭似乎微不足道，但它卻是一幢穩固持久的建築物的重要部分。

　　 a ) 真實的　　　　 b ) 微不足道的　　 c ) 堅固的　　　　 d ) 實體的

**題解**：文句中有一個 but，可得知空格的字義應該與 important 相對照，因此只有 b ) insignificant（微不足道的）符合題意。

## 2.

**答案**：c ) confident（自信的）

**中譯**：穿著合適的套裝，讓你看起來充滿自信，是工作面試的成功關鍵之一。

　　 a ) 能共處的　　　 b ) 緊密的　　　　　 c ) 自信的　　　　 d ) 蓬亂的

**題解**：由 successful job interview 推論穿著合適的套裝會有正面的影響，因此選 c ) confident（自信的）。

## 3.

**答案**：d ) suffering（遭受）

**中譯**：參與戶外活動時，請確保補充大量的水分。如果有任何人看似中暑，請帶他們前往緊急醫療中心。

a）預防　　　　b）犧牲　　　　c）相異　　　　d）遭受

題解：在需要前往緊急醫療站前，必定是因為遭受某種身體不適或受傷痛或不適，而由中暑 heat exhaustion 判斷，得知是 d）suffering（遭受）是最適合的答案。

# 4 - 1. ～ 4 - 2.

聽力原文：

Now we have had a lot of complaints about the lack of space and increased noise levels causing a lot of office stress. Let me first say, we're going to completely redo the cubicle layout this weekend and create more space for you all. The noise problem seems to be a case of either having the sound on your PC too loud, or shouting to others to get their attention. Remember, try to be considerate of others. If you have the sound up too loud, lower the volume a bit. If you need to talk to someone across the way, go over to their desk, please, before you yell across the room.

原文翻譯：

現在目前我們有很多人抱怨空間狹小以及不斷增加的噪音，造成很大的辦公壓力。請容我先說明，我們將在這週末重新隔間，並為你們創造更寬廣的空間。噪音的問題似乎是因為各位桌上型電腦的音效開得太大，或是為了吸引對方注意而對他人大聲呼喊。記得，請盡量體諒他人。若你造成的音量太大，請稍微降低一些音量。若你需要和另一邊的人講話，拜託，請在隔空呼喊前，走到他們的辦公桌旁邊。

# 4 - 1. 🎧 ......

答案：b）Use PCs more considerately.（更加體貼地使用電腦。）

中譯：文中建議了哪件事？

a) 保持辦公室整潔。　　　　b) 更加體貼地使用電腦。

c) 降低收音機的音量。　　　　d) 走過辦公室時保持安靜。

**題解：** 文中提到噪音來源之一為 having the sound on your PC too loud，說話者因此暗示了在使用電腦時必須更加體諒別人。

# 4 - 2. 🎧

**答案：** d) The office layout will be changed.（辦公室隔間將改變。）

**中譯：** 空間問題將會如何處理？

　　　　a) 一些辦公桌會被丟棄。

　　　　b) 將會買下另一棟大樓。

　　　　c) 將會多使用另一樓層。

　　　　d) 辦公室隔間將改變。

**題解：** 文中提到的 ...we're going to completely redo the cubicle layout this weekend and create more space for you all，由此得知為了增加使用空間，辦公室隔間將改變。

# 題解 6

## 1.

**答案**：c ) known（知名的）

**中譯**：Leonard 市長很驕傲地形容該城市是以居民的好客而聞名。

　　　　a ) 通知　　　　　b ) 譴責　　　　　c ) 知名的　　　　d ) 拿取

**題解**：從前面的 proudly described（驕傲地形容）可推論出後面接的應是正面的選項，因此 c ) 知名的，最符合要求。

## 2.

**答案**：c ) customers（顧客）

**中譯**：如果你把顧客視為朋友，他們很有可能會成為你公司產品或服務的擁護者。

　　　　a ) 競爭者　　　　b ) 風俗　　　　　c ) 顧客　　　　　d ) 託管人

**題解**：從句子後面：擁護公司產品和服務，可推論出前面接的應是 c ) 顧客。

## 3.

**答案**：a ) decrease（降低）

**中譯**：分析家認為失業率的降低是經濟復甦的跡象。

　　　　a ) 降低　　　　　b ) 得體　　　　　c ) 貶低　　　　　d ) 犯罪

**題解** ： 經濟復甦必須是失業率低，因此選項 a ) 降低失業率，最符合文意。

# 4 - 1. ～ 4 - 2.

**聽力原文：**

Robbery detectives were searching for clues today relating to the holdups of three banks in the West Hills area yesterday. The first heist occurred at 1:27 p.m. yesterday at First Federal Bank on Scottsdale Boulevard. While police were questioning witnesses, they received word of another robbery less than a mile away. At 4:20 p.m., police were called to Family Savings & Loan on Bellingham Way where a man in a red ski mask had run off with more than 3,200 dollars. Witnesses at each bank described the robber as a man in a red ski mask, about five feet and ten inches. Police believe the robberies are related.

**原文翻譯：**

警方正在調查昨天在 West Hills 地區發生的三起銀行持槍搶案。第一起搶案發生在昨天下午 1 點 27 分 Scottsdale Boulevard 的第一聯邦銀行。當警方正在詢問目擊者時，又得知不到一哩外發生另一起搶案。在下午 4 點 20 分警方又接獲報案，Bellingham Way 的 Family Savings & Loan 銀行有一個戴紅色滑雪面罩的男人搶走超過 3,200 元的金額。每家銀行的目擊者都描述搶匪是戴紅色滑雪面罩，約五呎十吋的男子。警方相信這些搶案應有關聯。

# 4 - 1.

**答案** ： d ) The descriptions of the robber were identical.
（對搶匪的描述相同。）

**中譯** ： 為何警方認為這些搶案有關聯？

a ) 被搶的銀行都在同一條街。

b ) 被搶的都是同一間銀行的分行 。

c ) 搶匪承認犯罪。

d ) 對搶匪的描述相同。

題解：倒數第二句提到，每家銀行的目擊者都描述搶匪是戴紅色滑雪面罩，因此可得知原因是 d ) 對搶匪的描述相同。

# 4 - 2.

答案：c ) In the afternoon（下午）

中譯：這些搶案何時發生？

a ) 早上

b ) 深夜

c ) 下午

d ) 傍晚

題解：文中提到兩個時間 1:27 p.m. 和 4:20 p.m. 因此可得知搶案是發生在 c ) 下午。

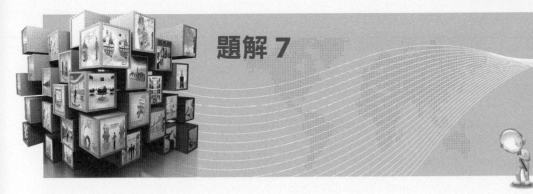

題解 **7**

## 1.

答案：c ) permission（許可）

中譯：根據新的門禁規定，實驗室的工作人員需要特殊許可才能進入研發部門。

　　a ) 禁止　　　　　b ) 承諾　　　　　c ) 許可　　　　　d ) 聲望

題解：因為是要 gain access to（進入）所以需要特殊的許可，選項 c ) permission 最符合
　　　文意。

## 2.

答案：b ) ideal（理想）

中譯：隨著公路網絡和鐵路貨運的連結，該國的東南部成為理想設立廠房的地點。

　　a ) 主意　　　　　b ) 理想　　　　　c ) 相同的　　　　d ) 意識型態的

題解：從前述的優點，公路網絡和鐵路貨運的連結可得知該地是設立廠房的最理想地點，
　　　因此選項 b ) 理想 最符合文意。

## 3.

答案：a ) Failure（失敗）

中譯：不能確保飲用水的來源，可能會讓該社區暴露於由飲水引發的
　　　傳染病中。

a）失敗　　　　　b）謬誤　　　　　c）幫助　　　　　d）虛構

**題解**：從句子後半的傳染病可推論出前面在確保飲用水來源時應該是失敗的，因此選 a）失敗。

# 4 - 1. ～ 4 - 2.

**聽力原文：**

Welcome to the Parson City Public Library guided tour. The tour begins at the first floor north entrance and should take approximately 30 minutes. Please follow along as I describe various aspects of our library. The Parson City Public Library first opened in 1974 and covers 40,000 square feet on three floors. Our current collection numbers over 250,000 titles, not including media and archives. These holdings include books, periodicals, reference and index volumes, dissertations, microforms and computer materials. Renovation and upgrades have provided us with more study and shelf space, more room for archives and more office space. On your left, you'll find the new Library Computer Lab. Our new networked computer lab has 30 fully functioning public workstations which give access to the computer catalogue, local and online databases and word processing software. A new security system has recently been installed. Professional, full-time, part-time and student workers compose the library work force to help provide the services and resources for all visitors to the library.

**原文翻譯：**

歡迎蒞臨 Parson 市立圖書館的導覽之旅。導覽將在一樓北邊入口處開始，歷時約 30 分鐘。請跟隨我，我會從各種角度講述圖書館。Parson 市立圖書館在 1974 年開幕，總面積 40,000 平方英呎，共三層樓高。我們目前的收藏品超過 250,000 件，不包含影音資料和存檔。這些收藏包括了書籍、期刊、參考索引目錄、學術論文、

226

微縮複製品和電腦資料。翻修和升級提供我們更多的研讀空間和書架位置，更多儲放檔案和辦公的地方。在你的左手邊，你會看到新的圖書館電腦室。我們新型的網路電腦室有三十個功能完整的公共工作站，提供了電子目錄、當地和線上的資料庫及文字處理軟體。最近也安裝了新的保全系統。圖書館的工作人員包含了專業人士、全職、兼職以及工讀生，都會為圖書館的所有訪客提供服務。

## 4 - 1.

答案：d）Computer discs（電腦光碟）

中譯：在 250,000 件收藏品中包含什麼？

　　　a）報紙　　　　　b）錄音帶　　　　c）錄影帶　　　　d）電腦光碟

題解：文中提到的有 ...computer materials... 因此只有選項 d）電腦光碟 有在範圍內。

## 4 - 2.

答案：a）Write reports.（寫報告）

中譯：你能在電腦室做什麼？

　　　a）寫報告。　　　b）玩電動。　　　c）發電子郵件。　　d）教電腦程式。

題解：文中提到電腦室提供了 ...word processing software( 文字處理軟體)... 因此可得知可以在電腦室裡 a）寫報告

# 題解 8

## 1.

答案：a ) investigation（調查）

中譯：法官已針對內線交易案，把 Annkor 集團總裁列入正式調查範圍。

    a ) 調查        b ) 利益        c ) 發明        d ) 投資

題解：從 judge（法官）、probe（全面調查）可以判斷出 a ) investigation（調查）最符合文意。

## 2.

答案：b ) Internet（網路）

中譯：這位巨星的驟逝已造成網路壅塞，因為數以百萬的人登入電腦，搜尋線上相關資訊。

    a ) 介面        b ) 網路        c ) 互動        d ) 間歇

題解：從 computer（電腦）、information online（線上資訊）可以判斷出相關字應是 b ) Internet（網路）。

## 3.

答案：a ) damage（損害）

中譯：帳戶被轉移到催收公司名單中，可能會損害你的信用紀錄，並影響你在未來五年內再度貸款的能力。

a）損害　　　　　b）使受益　　　　c）衰退　　　　d）裝飾

**題解**：列入催收公司名單內對於信用紀錄是有害的，因此選項 a）damage（損害）最符合文意。

# 4 - 1. ～ 4 - 2.

**聽力原文：**

All this week at Sherman's Supermarket, we are having a sale to help you prepare for Easter. We know your children are looking forward to dyeing Easter eggs, so we have conveniently placed egg-painting supplies next to the dairy and eggs refrigerated cases. And at the front of the store, you will notice our display of Easter candies and chocolates, some on sale for up to 50 percent off. Finally, get stocked up for your Easter feast, starting with one of our glazed hams in the meat department. All glazed hams from any one of the three brands we carry are 20 percent off.

**原文翻譯：**

Sherman 超市整週都有折扣以便各位準備復活節。我們知道您的小孩很期待塗復活節彩蛋，因此貼心地為您把彩蛋的工具放在乳製品和雞蛋的冷藏櫃隔壁。在店面的前方有復活節糖果和巧克力的陳列，有些甚至到五折的優惠。最後，為了讓您的復活節大餐更豐盛，請參考我們肉品區具光澤的火腿。任選我們販賣的三個廠牌之一都是八折。

# 4 - 1. 🎧 ⋯⋯⋯⋯⋯⋯⋯⋯⋯⋯⋯⋯⋯⋯⋯⋯⋯

**答案**：b）Moved the paints next to the egg case.（把顏料移到蛋盒旁）

**中譯**：商店為想要畫復活節彩蛋的人做了什麼？

a）把蛋移到顏料旁          b）把顏料移到蛋盒旁

c）顏料半價優惠          d）蛋每盒促銷價 1.5 美元

**題解：**文中提到 ...placed egg-painting supplies next to the dairy and eggs refrigerated cases... 因此可得知是 b）Moved the paints next to the egg case.（把顏料移到蛋盒旁）。

# 4 - 2. 🎧 ...........................................................................................

**答案：**d）Some of the Easter candy（部分的復活節糖果）

**中譯：**什麼東西是半價？

a）具光澤的火腿          b）所有在蛋和乳製品區的東西

c）所有復活節糖果          d）部分的復活節糖果

**題解：**文中提到 ...Easter candies and chocolates, some on sale for up to 50 percent off, 因此可得知半價的是 d）部分的復活節糖果。

# 題解 9

## 1.

**答案**：a ) edible（可食用的）

**中譯**：這是可食用的植物，但除非經過仔細地烹調，否則你將會生病。

　　　　a ) 可食用的　　　　b ) 難以閱讀的　　　c ) 合適的　　　　d ) 和藹可親的

**題解**：從 cooked well（仔細烹調）可以判斷出應與吃有關，所以選項 a ) edible（可食用的）
　　　　最符合文意。

## 2.

**答案**：b ) activated（啟用）

**中譯**：為了保護信用卡持卡人的權益，除非從持卡人家用電話啟用，否則不能使用卡片。

　　　　a ) 使無效　　　　b ) 啟用　　　　c ) 同意　　　　d ) 取消

**題解**：從文意判斷保護措施是限制必須用持卡人家用電話，所以使用卡片是選項 b )
　　　　activated（啟用）最符合文意。

## 3.

**答案**：c ) otherwise（另）

**中譯**：以下的規範適用於所有層級的聯賽，除非另有明確規定。

a ) 除了          b ) 而不是          c ) 另          d ) 別處

題解 : 從前面的 apply to all（適用於所有）可判斷出若有例外，應是要另外的特別規定，所以選項 c ) otherwise（另）最符合文意。

## 4.

聽力原文 :

M : The power company just called. They threatened to cut off our electricity unless we pay the bill.

W : When was it due?

M : Last Wednesday!

原文翻譯 :

男：電力公司剛打來。他們威脅要切斷我們的電力除非我們繳帳單。

女：繳費期限是什麼時候？

男：上星期三！

答案 : b ) Last week（上星期）

中譯 : 帳單何時就應該要付？

　　　　a ) 一個月以前　　b ) 上星期　　c ) 兩週前　　d ) 昨天

題解 : 文中提到上週三就應該要付款，所以答案是 b ) Last week（上星期）。

## 5.

聽力原文 :

M : The guidebook recommends we go to Antonio's if we want Italian.

W : That's fine with me, unless you want to get Chinese or order some room service.

M : I'm not really in the mood for Chinese, and I want to go out tonight.

原文翻譯：

男：如果想吃義大利菜，旅行指南推薦我們去 Antonio 餐廳。

女：我可以接受，除非你想吃中國菜或點客房服務。

男：我不是很想吃中國菜，而且我今晚想出門。

**答案**：b) At Antonio's（在 Antonio 餐廳。）

**中譯**：他們最可能在哪裡吃晚餐？

a) 在他們的房間裡　　　　　　　b) 在 Antonio 餐廳

c) 在俄國餐廳　　　　　　　　　d) 在中國餐廳

**題解**：男士最後的回答是不想吃中國菜而且要出門吃，因此可推論出他們會去吃義大利菜，所以是選項 b) At Antonio's（在 Antonio 餐廳）。

# 題解 10

## 1.

**答案**：a ) defective（有缺點的）

**中譯**：若發現產品有瑕疵，消費者除了應把產品和其保證書帶回原購物處，還要帶產品購買的收據。

　　a ) 有缺點的　　　　　b ) 完美的　　　　　c ) 正派的　　　　　d ) 可行的

**題解**：從文意判斷要將產品帶回購買處應是產品出問題，所以是選項 a ) defective（有缺點的）。

## 2.

**答案**：d ) discipline（紀律）

**中譯**：分期付款除了要有財務上的紀律還要有足夠的金錢。

　　a ) 信徒　　　　　b ) 歧見　　　　　c ) 討論　　　　　d ) 紀律

**題解**：分期付款需要長期的穩定償還，因此選項 d ) discipline（紀律）是重要的還款要件。

## 3.

**答案**：c ) quantity（量）

**中譯**：若員工能團隊合作並從同儕間學習，所有成員整體的技能表現將有所不同，在質與量方面都會改變。

a）引述 　　　　b）行列 　　　　c）量 　　　　d）四合院

**題解**：與空格相對應的是 quality（質），因此可推論出應為 c）quantity（量）。

# 4 - 1. ～ 4 - 2.

**聽力原文：**

Good evening, and welcome to tonight's edition of *Finance in Review*. Tonight we will be talking to Edward Richardson, who is head of Metropolitan Banking Group, as well as member of the board of trustees for Anarco Steel Corporation. He has received the Jackson Award for excellence in the field of economic effects of globalization on medium-sized corporations. Tonight he will be discussing recent important changes in the global economy.

**原文翻譯：**

晚安並歡迎您蒞臨今晚這期的《財經回顧》。今晚我們將會和 Metropolitan 金融集團的總裁 Edward Richardson 先生進行對談，他同時也是 Anarco 鋼鐵公司理事會的成員。他研究全球化對中型企業的經濟影響，因為在該領域的傑出成就，而獲頒 Jackson 獎項。今晚他將會討論最近在全球經濟上的重要轉變。

# 4 - 1.

**答案**：a）A banking group（金融集團）

**中譯**：Edward Richardson 是哪個領域面的總裁？

a）金融集團 　　　　　　　　b）鋼鐵公司

c）經濟學領域 　　　　　　　d）一家中型企業

**題解**：文中提到他是 ...head of Metropolitan Banking Group...，因此可得知是選項 a）A banking group（金融集團）。

**答案**：d）His ideas on the effects of globalization（他對全球化影響的想法）

**中譯**：Edward Richardson 是因何而授予獎項？

　　a）他對自己公司的說明　　　　　　b）他對政治的熱情

　　c）他出席《財經回顧》的場合　　　d）他對全球化影響的想法

**題解**：文中提到該獎項是獎勵在全球化經濟效益有傑出表現的中型企業，所以選項 d）His ideas on the effects of globalization（他對全球化影響的想法）最符合文意。

# 題解 11

## 1.

**答案**：a ) information（資訊）

**中譯**：若你正在找尋島嶼冒險，我們的服務台很樂意提供你許多關於 Maui 戶外活動的資訊。

a ) 資訊　　　　b ) 通知者　　　　c ) 陰謀　　　　d ) 遊客

**題解**：從 concierge desk（服務台）可以判斷出那是提供旅客資訊的地方，因此選項 a ) information（資訊）最符合文意。

## 2.

**答案**：c ) disclose（公開）

**中譯**：有鑑於最近的金融危機，壽險公司應該提供客戶年報，以公開保單現金價值的投資報酬率。

a ) 隱藏　　　　b ) 恢復　　　　c ) 公開　　　　d ) 關閉

**題解**：因為金融危機，壽險公司為了讓客戶放心，應主動將資訊公開，因此選項 c ) disclose（公開）最符合文意。

## 3.

**答案**：a ) progress（前進）

**中譯**：你或許不想成為侍者或售貨員，但這些基層工作是你邁向高階職位的必備墊腳石。

      a ) 前進            b ) 舉起            c ) 增加            d ) 提升

**題解**：從 entry-level jobs（基層工作）到 higher positions（高階職位）可推論出是一項往前進的過程，因此選項 a ) progress（前進）最符合文意。

# 4 - 1. ～ 4 - 2.

**聽力原文**：

Sixty-Second Rental Cars is here to provide you with the driving experience of a lifetime. We provide luxury and exotic automobile rentals at four convenient locations in the Los Angeles area. We feature almost every top-of-the-line car imaginable as well as a full line of sport-utility vehicles and luxury sedans. We promise the most diverse selection and the best service in the country. And during this special campaign, 50 people will have the chance of winning a two-night stay at the five-star Hotel Imperial. Please check our Website for details at www.sixty-secondrental.com.

**原文翻譯**：

六十秒租車公司提供提供您此生夢寐以求的駕駛經驗。我們在洛杉磯四個據點提供承租豪華與外來車種。我們的特色是擁有幾乎所有想像得到的頂級車種，此外還有全系列越野休閒車種和豪華房車。我們保證有最多樣的選擇和國內最棒的服務。在優惠活動期間，將有五十個名額有機會入住兩晚 Imperial 五星級飯店。請上我們的網站 www.sixty-secondrental.com 查詢更多細節。

## 4 - 1.

**答案：** b ) Its variety of rental car choices（租車選擇的多樣性）

**中譯：** 這間公司自豪之處在於？

　　a ) 具競爭力的價格　　　　　　　b ) 租車選擇的多樣性

　　c ) 全國性的生意　　　　　　　　d ) 到機場的便捷性

**題解：** 文中提到 ...We promise the most diverse selection, 因此可得知它自豪的是 b ) Its variety of rental car choices（租車選擇的多樣性）。

## 4 - 2.

**答案：** c ) A free stay at a luxury hotel（豪華飯店的免費住宿）

**中譯：** 客戶可能在這項優惠活動中贏得什麼？

　　a ) 租車折扣　　　　　　　　　　b ) 到洛杉磯的機票

　　c ) 豪華飯店的免費住宿　　　　　d ) 飯店的折價券

**題解：** 文末提到 ...winning a two-night stay at the five-star Hotel, 因此可得知獎項是 c ) A free stay at a luxury hotel（豪華飯店的免費住宿）。

## 題解 12

**1.**

**答案：** a) evidence（證據）

**中譯：** 沒有證據顯示，基因改造作物和食品有毒性或會造成過敏。

　　a)證據　　　　　　b)程式　　　　　　c)助理　　　　　　d)進入

**題解：** 基因改造食物有無毒性並未獲得證實，因此選項 a) evidence（證據）最符合文意。
　　　　GM：gene modified（基因改造）

**2.**

**答案：** a) highlight（凸顯）

**中譯：** 這些健身計畫毫無疑問地凸顯出積極生活的重要性，並鼓勵社群的參與。

　　a)凸顯　　　　　　b)強迫　　　　　　c)要求　　　　　　d)懇求

**題解：** 從 active lifestyle（積極的生活態度）和 encourage community involvement（鼓勵社區參與）等字義可判斷出 a) highlight（凸顯）最符合文意。

**3.**

**答案：** c) suggest（顯示）

**中譯：** 沒有任何證據顯示使用手機或筆電是造成最近飛安事故的原因。

　　a)陳述　　　　　　b)領悟　　　　　　c)顯示　　　　　　d)突出

題解：手機與飛安事故並未被證實有直接關聯，因此選項 c）suggest（顯示）最符合文意。

# 4 - 1. ～ 4 - 2.

**聽力原文：**

Ladies and Gentlemen, you have been gathered here today as possible members of the jury for this criminal case. However, first we must learn a little bit about you to determine if you are eligible for jury duty here in the state of Texas. You will be asked a series of questions regarding any number of subjects, such as whether you are registered to vote or not, if you have ever been in jail, if you have ever been diagnosed as insane, or if you have any relation to the parties involved in this case. Please answer the questions truthfully.

**原文翻譯：**

各位先生女士，今天聚集在這裡的原因是您可能成為這起罪案的陪審團成員。然而，我們必須先稍微瞭解各位以決定您是否有資格成為德州的陪審團。您將會被問到以下有關的一連串問題，例如您是否有投票權、是否入獄過、是否曾被診斷為精神失常、或是與該罪案成員有任何關聯。請據實回答這些問題。

# 4 - 1.

**答案**：b）To be selected for some duty（為履行某些職責受選）

**中譯**：聽眾聚集的原因是？

　　　a）為犯罪訴訟受審　　　　　b）為履行某些職責受選

　　　c）選出陪審團代表　　　　　d）學習陪審團的歷史

**題解**：從文中提到 ...as possible members of the jury（陪審團的可能成員）及 ...determine if you are eligible for jury duty（決定是

否有資格成為陪審員）可推論出聚集的原因是要被選上陪審員，所以選項 b ) To be selected for some duty（為履行某些職責受選）最符合文意。

# 4 - 2. 🎧 .....................................................................................................................

**答案：** d ) Answer a series of questions.（回答一連串的問題。）

**中譯：** 在講完話後他們會做什麼？

　　　a ) 介紹他們自己。　　　　　　　　b ) 登記投票。

　　　c ) 寫短文。　　　　　　　　　　　d ) 回答一連串的問題。

**題解：** 文中提到 ...will be asked a series of questions，因此可得知聽眾之後會 d ) Answer a series of questions.（回答一連串的問題。）

# Operations
# 商務運作

# 題解 1

## 1.

**答案**：d ) evacuation（撤離）

**中譯**：住在低窪地區的居民正準備要撤離，因為很有可能會潰堤。

    a ) 展覽            b ) 解釋            c ) 免除            d ) 撤離

**題解**：因為潰堤的可能性，所以低窪地區的居民必須要 d ) 撤離。

## 2.

**答案**：c ) hair nets（髮網）

**中譯**：頭髮很有可能在移動的生產線上被纏住，所以靠近生產線時必須隨時戴著髮網。

    a ) 接髮            b ) 髮膠            c ) 髮網            d ) 髮型

**題解**：因為頭髮可能被纏住，所以必須戴 c ) 髮網 以策安全。

## 3.

**答案**：a ) deteriorating（惡化）

**中譯**：更密閉的結構以及內裝材料變得更加化學合成，因而可能惡化室內空氣品質。

    a ) 惡化            b ) 增加            c ) 進行            d ) 改善

**題解**：因為前述的缺點：密閉的結構和化學合成材料，導致室內空氣品質會 a ) 惡化。

# 4 - 1. ～ 4 - 2.

**聽力原文：**

With the recent scandal surrounding teen idol Shawn Holland, society is again forced to think about what effect public figures have on its sense of morality. This becomes even more problematic when the public figure, revered by millions of young people, is a very young person himself so therefore more likely to make immature, bad decisions. It is possible that this sort of scandal will have little effect on our youth as a whole, but I think not. It is my belief that this type of thing is ultimately destructive for how our youth judges between what is good or bad.

**原文翻譯：**

因為最近年輕偶像 Shawn Holland 醜聞纏身，社會被迫再次思考公眾人物對社會道德所帶來的影響。這位被數百萬年輕人崇拜的公眾人物本身也很年輕，他很有可能會做出不成熟的決定，這將會產生更大的問題。這類的醜聞或許對我們的青少年整體影響不大，但我不這麼認為。我相信這類事件最終會破壞青少年判斷好壞的準則。

# 4 - 1.

**答案：** d ) That scandals involving teen idols are bad for morality

（年輕偶像的醜聞對道德有不好的影響）

**中譯：** 演說者最後做出什麼結論？

a ) 社會被迫思考道德問題

b ) 年輕人總是做出好的決定

c ) 公眾醜聞不會影響年輕人

d ) 年輕偶像的醜聞對道德有不好的影響

**題解**：文章最後提到：我相信這類事件最終會破壞青少年判斷好壞的標準，所以選項 d )
年輕偶像的醜聞對道德有不好的影響，最符合文意。

# 4 - 2. 🎧 ...........................................................................................................................

**答案**：a ) The effect of famous people on the morals of society.
（名人對社會道德的影響力）

**中譯**：這起事件讓社會大眾去思考什麼？

a ) 名人對社會道德的影響力

b ) 缺乏對整體青少年的影響

c ) 年輕偶像 Shawn Holland 受歡迎的程度

d ) 多少人每天想著年輕偶像

**題解**：文中第二句提到 ...what effect public figures have on its sense of morality 因此選項
a ) 名人對社會道德的影響力 才是社會要思考的地方。

# 題解 2

## 1.

**答案**：c) maintaining（維持）

**中譯**：LLC 企業致力於提供最佳的產品及服務，同時又維持高品質及可負擔的價格。

a) 犧牲　　　　b) 彌補　　　　c) 維持　　　　d) 索價

**題解**：由 while 得知 highest level of performance 和 quality and affordability 必須同時兼顧，因此答案為 maintaining（維持）。

## 2.

**答案**：a) pursuing（追求 V-ing）

**中譯**：如果你想投入表演事業，你必須先擁有學習表演技能的熱情及動力。

a) 追求（V- ing）　b) 追求（名詞）　c) 提議　　　　d) 追求（過去式）

**題解**：committed "to" 後面加 V-ing 或名詞，只有 a) pursuing 符合句意及文法結構。

## 3.

**答案**：b) development（開發）

**中譯**：Spine Align 致力於開發高品質、創新的醫療器材以醫治脊椎不適。

a) 破壞　　　　b) 開發　　　　c) 神聖的　　　　d) 嘲弄

題解： 由 high-quality innovative medical devices for the treatment of spinal disorders 得
知目的，因而需要去「開發、研發」。

# 4. 🎧 ........................................................................................................

**聽力原文：**

M：My friend is learning Portuguese so she can go to Brazil and volunteer there.

W：That's great! She must be really dedicated to helping other people.

M：Yeah, and it's also a good way for her to follow her other passion, which is traveling.

**原文翻譯：**

男：我的朋友為了要去巴西參與志工活動正在學葡萄牙文。

女：太好了！她一定非常致力於幫助他人。

男：沒錯，而且這也是她追求另一項熱忱的好方法，也就是到處旅遊。

答案： a) Because she wants to travel and aid people in need

（因為她想旅遊並幫助需要的人）

中譯： 為什麼該男士的朋友在學習葡萄牙文？

a) 因為她想旅遊並幫助需要的人

b) 因為她想旅遊並成為語言專家

c) 因為她想幫助她自己的國人

d) 因為她想教授葡萄牙文並幫助小孩子

題解： 由 go to Brazil and volunteer there 以及 it's also a good way for her to follow her
other passion, which is traveling 得知要去擔任志工，同時又能旅遊。

# 題解 3

## 1.

**答案**：c ) traffic（流量）

**中譯**：為了增加他部落格的流量，Nick 決定在其他部落格發表評論。

  a ) 網路　　　　　　　b ) 提及　　　　　　c ) 流量　　　　　　d ) 推測

**題解**：從 drive more...to his blog 可看出只有 c ) traffic（流量）符合句意。

## 2.

**答案**：b ) activate（啟動）

**中譯**：為了啟動您的網路帳戶，您必須為您的 Master Username 帳號設置密碼。

  a ) 打開　　　　　　b ) 啟動　　　　　　c ) 打斷　　　　　d ) 介紹

**題解**：由 account online，和 password 推知，答案為 b ) activate（啟動）。

## 3.

**答案**：b ) reduce（減低）

**中譯**：我們必須執行一些有意義的解決方案，以減低日常生活中的石油
消耗量。

  a ) 產生　　　　　　b ) 減低　　　　　c ) 誘惑　　　　　d ) 導致

**題解**：從線索字 consumption 可得知，只有 b ) reduce（減低）符合句意。

# 4 - 1. ～ 4 - 2.

**聽力原文：**

Over the next couple of days, we are going to do a series of exercises ranging from sitting and breathing, to snorkel diving, to your first actual dive with scuba gear. These exercises are designed to build up your confidence, as well as give you a foundation of knowledge that will ensure your safety in future dives. Has everyone signed the permission waiver? That is necessary in order to proceed with the instruction. Now, if that is out of the way, let's begin by learning about all the equipment you will eventually be using.

**原文翻譯：**

在未來幾天，我們將做一系列的練習，從坐、呼吸、浮潛，到第一次實際穿戴潛水呼吸器潛水。這些練習的目的是建立你的信心，以及灌輸你基本知識，以便未來潛水時，確保你自身的安全。各位都簽訂切結書了嗎？這是必要的，以進行技術指導。現在，如果沒有其他問題，讓我們先來瞭解所有最終將使用到的設備。

## 4 - 1. 🎧

**答案：** b ) A few days（幾天）

**中譯：** 這個課程將會進行多久？

　　　a ) 幾小時　　　　b ) 幾天　　　　c ) 幾週　　　　d ) 幾個月

**題解：** 由一開始 Over the next couple of days，推知是幾天。

## 4 - 2. 🎧

**答案：** c ) To learn to scuba dive in safety（學習安全潛水）

中譯：這堂課程的目的為何？

　　　a ) 要成為潛水設備專家

　　　b ) 學習在任何類型的氣候下潛水

　　　c ) 學習安全潛水

　　　d ) 學習同心協力潛水

題解：由 These exercises are designed to build up your confidence, as well as give you a foundation of knowledge that will ensure your safety in future dives. 得知是安全潛水。

# 題解 4

## 1.

**答案**：c) purpose（目的）

**中譯**：這項任務的目的是要幫助你應用各式相關的心理壓力模式。

　　　a) 議程　　　　　b) 評論　　　　　c) 目的　　　　　d) 困境

**題解**：句子後段已說明目的，因次可得知這些說明是在敘述這項任務 this assignment 的目的，所以選項 c) purpose（目的）最符合文意。

## 2.

**答案**：c) investigation（調查）

**中譯**：這項調查的目的是為了確認漏油的情形有多嚴重以及偵察油類的成份，以便正確控制情勢。

　　　a) 投資　　　　　b) 整合　　　　　c) 調查　　　　　d) 審問

**題解**：從 determine 和 detect 可得知是要查出事情的狀況，因此選項 c) investigation（調查）較符合文意。

## 3.

**答案**：a) discover（發掘）

中譯：這篇論文的主要目的是發掘治療血癌的各種自然療法背後的真相。

　　　a）發掘　　　　　b）打開　　　　　c）隱藏　　　　　d）偽造

題解：從 truth 可得知論文的主要目的是為了發現真相，因此 a）discover（發掘）最符合
　　　文意。

# 4 - 1. ～ 4 - 2.

**聽力原文：**

The new Outdoorsman Truck was created with pure practicality in mind. Its one-ton body has been designed for durability with the most advanced engineering available and an extra-wide wheelbase for stability and safety. It has four-wheel drive with a four-liter engine, providing spectacular power for any and all hauling needs. Yet even with all this power, it has been designed so ingeniously that it gets 18 miles per gallon in the city, and 22 miles per gallon on the highway. Test-drive the new Outdoorsman Truck at your local dealer.

**原文翻譯：**

新型的 Outdoorsman 卡車設計時以真正的實用性出發。它一噸重的車體以最先進的工程技術打造其耐久性，特殊加寬的軸距也確保了穩定度和安全性。Outdoorsman 卡車有四輪傳動並具備四公升引擎，為任何拖運的需求提供驚人的動力。除了這些動力之外，精巧的設計使其在城市每加侖油可跑 18 英里，在高速公路上可跑 22 英里。快到當地的經銷商試開全新的 Outdoorsman 卡車吧。

# 4 -1.

答案：b）Stability（穩定度）

中譯：特殊加寬的軸距有何用意？

　　　a）速度　　　　　b）穩定度　　　　　c）時尚感　　　　　d）耐久度

**題解**： 文中第二句提到 ...an extra-wide wheelbase for stability and safety... 因此可得知特殊加寬的軸距是為了穩定度，因此 b ) Stability（穩定度）最符合文意。

# 4 - 2. 🎧 ················································································

**答案**： c ) A 4-wheel drive system and 4-liter engine.（四輪傳動系統和四公升引擎）

**中譯**： 是何種裝置讓卡車擁有引人注目的動力？

　　　　a ) 全然的實用性

　　　　b ) 耐久的一噸重車身

　　　　c ) 四輪傳動系統和四公升引擎

　　　　d ) 獨創設計的駕駛裝置

**題解**： 文後半段有提到 ...four-wheel drive with a four-liter engine, providing spectacular power... 因此可得知動力特色中最引人注目的是 c ) A 4-wheel drive system and 4-liter engine（四輪傳動系統和四公升引擎）。

# 題解 5

## 1.

**答案**：c ) charge（索價）

**中譯**：EBK 航空會對過重的乘客索價兩個位置的費用，否則可能不允許他們登機。

　　　a ) 支付　　　　　b ) 增加　　　　　c ) 索價　　　　　d ) 花費

**題解**：由句中的 for two seats（兩個位置）推論應與付費有關，因此選項 c ) charge（索價）最符合文意。

## 2.

**答案**：d ) discounted（折扣）

**中譯**：國道收費管理處會給共乘的旅客 $2.50 的優待過路費，以減少交通壅塞。

　　　a ) 感激　　　　　b ) 提升　　　　　c ) 分辨　　　　　d ) 折扣

**題解**：由文意判斷共乘的旅客對交通有幫助，因此收費處應會給予優待，所以是選項 d ) discounted（折扣）。

## 3.

**答案**：a ) account（帳戶）

**中譯**：若可以把消費帳單列計到飯店房費帳戶，人們更有可能會在飯店內消費。

a ) 帳戶　　　　　b ) 一致　　　　　c ) 途徑　　　　　d ) 接受

題解：從 purchase（購買） 和 charge（索價） 可以判斷出應與金錢有關，因此選項 a )
account（帳戶）最符合文意。

## 4. 🎧

**聽力原文：**

Do we need to separate the paper from the plastic?

a ) I think we should go together to save on fuel.

b ) If we don't, the waste company will charge us a lot of money.

c ) I would rather drink out of a glass cup.

**原文翻譯：**

我們需要把紙和塑膠分類嗎？

a ) 我想我們應該一起去以節省燃料。

b ) 如果我們不分類，回收公司會向我們索取很多費用。

c ) 我寧可用玻璃杯喝水。

**答案**：b ) If we don't, the waste company will charge us a lot of money.

　　　　（如果我們不分類，回收公司會向我們索取很多費用。）

**題解**：因為問的是分類，所以只有選項 b ) 最符合文意。

## 5. 🎧

**聽力原文：**

When are paychecks issued?

a ) You should be charged at the end of the month.

b ) They are handed out every two weeks.

c ) Accounting is closed every other Monday.

## 原文翻譯：

薪水什麼時候核發？

a ) 你在月底會被收款。

b ) 每兩週發放。

c ) 隔週一會計關帳。

**答案**：b ) They are handed out every two weeks.（每兩週發放。）

**題解**：問句是什麼時候核發，只有 b ) They are handed out every two weeks.（每兩週發放。）最符合文意。

# 題解 6

## 1.

**答案**：a) charity（慈善）

**中譯**：一些著名的癌症倖存者準備要成立一個慈善基金會，在經濟上協助無法獲得及時醫療的高風險婦女。

　　a) 慈善　　　　　　b) 專題研討會　　　c) 草稿　　　　　　d) 活動

**題解**：句末主旨是要幫助無法及時獲得醫療的婦女，因此應填具慈善意味的單字，選項 a) charity（慈善）最符合文意。

## 2.

**答案**：c) tour（旅遊）

**中譯**：Mason 旅行社推出了假日的亞洲低價旅遊，引起其他旅行社紛紛仿效。

　　a) 運輸　　　　　　b) 傳送　　　　　c) 旅遊　　　　　　d) 時尚

**題解**： 由句末的 travel agencies（旅行社）可推論出該公司推出的也是旅遊行程，因此選項 c) tour（旅遊）最符合文意。

## 3.

**答案**：b) against（反對）

中譯：醫療聯盟藉由提高人們對抽菸的危害認識，推出一項反菸的活動。

　　　a）為了　　　　　　b）反對　　　　　c）在……期間　　　d）在……之上

題解：從句末的 harmful effect（有害的影響）可得知醫療聯盟應是反對抽菸的。因此選
　　　項 b）against（反對）最符合文意。

# 4 - 1. ～ 4 - 2.

**聽力原文：**

Thank you for coming to the Country Rotary Club meeting today. Before starting my speech, I'd like to give you a quick reminder. The club will be having its 22nd annual Country Rotary Club Dance Party here on December 18, exactly one week before Christmas Day. Tickets are 25 dollars per person and all profits go directly to buying Christmas presents for children in foster homes. To purchase tickets, please go to the reception desk. Each club member is allowed to purchase a maximum of four tickets. We hope to see you all there.

**原文翻譯：**

感謝您今天蒞臨鄉村扶輪社會議。在開始我的演說之前，我希望先提醒您，本社將在 12 月 18 日，聖誕節前一週在這裡舉行第 22 屆鄉村扶輪社年度舞會。門票是每人 25 美元且所有盈餘都將用來購買寄養家庭的孩子們的聖誕禮物。請到服務檯購票。每位社員最多可以買四張票。我們竭誠希望各位的光臨。

# 4 - 1. 🎧

答案：a）Seven days before Christmas（聖誕節前七天）

中譯：舞會何時舉行？

　　　a）聖誕節前七天　　　　　　　b）聖誕夜

　　　c）一週後　　　　　　　　　　d）12 月 22 號

**題解**：文中提到 ...exactly one week before Christmas Day.（聖誕節前一週），因此可得知舞會是在 a ) Seven days before Christmas（聖誕節前七天）。

# 4 - 2.

**答案**：d ) To collect money to benefit children（為孩童福利募款）

**中譯**：為何要舉辦舞會？

　　a ) 慶祝新年

　　b ) 聯絡社區感情

　　c ) 鞏固會員的關係

　　d ) 為孩童福利募款

**題解**：文中提到 ...all profits go directly to buying Christmas presents for children in foster homes 因此可得知該舞會目的是 d ) To collect money to benefit children（為孩童福利募款）。

# 題解 7

## 1.

**答案**：d) stable（穩定的）

**中譯**：保守派預估這家公司的財務狀況在調查期間仍會維持穩定。

　　a) 權威性的　　　　b) 被總結的　　　　c) 被審查的　　　　d) 穩定的

**題解**：形容公司的財務狀況，只有選項 d) stable（穩定的）較符合文意。

## 2.

**答案**：c) motivated（有積極性的）

**中譯**：維持員工的積極性是任何組織都可以做到的。

　　a) 受挫的　　　　b) 單調的　　　　c) 有積極性的　　　　d) 感動的

**題解**：從 ...something positive（積極的事）可以判斷出應為 c) motivated（有積極性的）。

## 3.

**答案**：c) tuned（收聽）

**中譯**：提醒您今明兩天要繼續收聽 NPR 新聞，以獲得海地地震的最新情形。

　　a) 冷靜　　　　b) 清醒　　　　c) 收聽　　　　d) 僵化

**題解**：為了要獲得最新消息必須收聽新聞，所以選項 c) tuned（收聽）最符合文意。

# 4 - 1. ～ 4 - 3.

**聽力原文：**

May I have your attention please; this is your captain speaking. We are currently experiencing quite a bit of turbulence due to a tropical storm due east of our flight route. There is nothing to be alarmed about, as we should be flying past this shortly. In the meantime, however, as it will be bumpy, please remain seated with your seatbelts fastened and please turn off all electronic devices. Flight attendants must also be seated at this time. They will be of assistance to you in just a few moments. Thank you.

**原文翻譯：**

請各位注意，我是機長。因為在我們的飛行路徑東方有一個熱帶風暴，我們現正經過很多亂流。各位不需驚慌，我們將會很快的穿過這個風暴。與此同時，可能會有些顛簸，請留在座位上並繫緊安全帶，關閉所有電子儀器。空服員也必須就座。稍後才能為您服務。謝謝。

# 4 - 1. 🎧 ......

**答案**：b ) In an airplane（飛機）

**中譯**：這則廣播最可能在哪裡發生？

　　　　a ) 遊樂場　　　　b ) 飛機　　　　　c ) 遊輪　　　　　d ) 熱帶地區

**題解**：從 captain（機長）、flight(飛行)、Flight attendants（空服員）等字可以判斷出這應是 b ) In an airplane（飛機）上的廣播。

# 4 - 2. 🎧 ......

**答案**：b ) For a short time（很短暫的時間）

中譯：現況會維持多久？

　　　a）無法得知

　　　b）很短暫的時間

　　　c）好幾個小時

　　　d）直到風暴停止

題解：文中提到 we should be flying past this shortly（將會很快的穿過風暴），因此可得知現狀會維持 b）For a short time（很短暫的時間）。

# 4 - 3.

答案：a）Sit down.（坐下。）

中譯：聽者必須做什麼？

　　　a）坐下。

　　　b）把人們固定。

　　　c）停止供餐。

　　　d）協助機長。

題解：機長要求大家 ...remain seated（坐在位置上）因此可得知聽者必須 a）Sit down.（坐下）。

# 題解 8

## 1.

**答案**：c ) illness（疾病）

**中譯**：使用健身房的員工，比較能放鬆，也更具生產力，而且因為生病請假的天數也減少了。

　　a ) 快樂　　　　　　b ) 規律性　　　　　c ) 疾病　　　　　d ) 運動

**題解**：題目中的 more relaxed and productive 說明員工使用健身房的成效，因此才會有「因為生病」請假的天數減少。

## 2.

**答案**：b ) difference（差異）

**中譯**：因為時差，在亞洲及南美的員工，必須在正常工作時間外上班。

　　a ) 均等　　　　　　b ) 差異　　　　　c ) 貨幣　　　　　d ) 流暢

**題解**：題目中的 in Asia and South America 及 outside of regular business hours 提供答題的線索，「因為時差」使位於不同地理區域的員工，必須在正常工時以外時間上班。

## 3.

**答案**：c ) favorable（適合的）

中譯：因為氣候適宜，加州具備生產蔬果的優勢。

　　a）有用的　　　　b）有害的　　　　c）適合的　　　　d）有價值的

題解：從 advantage 這個線索字得知，只有 favorable 符合句意。

# 4 - 1. ～ 4 - 2.

**聽力原文：**

May I have your attention, please? This is your captain speaking. Our scheduled arrival time for Ellis County Airport will be delayed a bit as the area is experiencing heavy thunderstorms. We will be in a holding pattern as we wait for the thunderstorms to pass. As we may run into some turbulence, please note that the seat belt sign is now turned on. Please remain seated with your seat belts fastened, and please turn off all portable electronic devices, including personal stereos and laptop computers. We expect we'll be on the ground within half an hour to 45 minutes.

**原文翻譯：**

大家請注意，現在是機長廣播，我們原訂到達 Ellis 郡的時間要稍微延後，因為該地區正下著大雷雨，我們將維持在航行狀態，等雷雨通過。由於我們會碰到一些亂流，請注意目前座位安全帶的燈號是亮著的，請大家坐在位子上，繫好您的安全帶，同時請關掉所有隨身攜帶的電子設備，包括個人音響及筆電。我們希望能在半小時至四十五分鐘之內降落。

# 4 - 1. 🎧

答案：b）To announce a landing delay due to bad weather

　　　（因為天候不佳，宣布延後降落）

中譯：為何要做這項宣布？

　　　a）因為意外事故，宣布延後降落

　　　b）因為天候不佳，宣布延後降落

　　　c）通知大家飛機即將下降

　　　d）通知大家即將上餐點

題解：文中提到 Our scheduled arrival time for Ellis County Airport will be delayed a bit as the area is experiencing heavy thunderstorms. 由此可知是因為天候不佳導致飛機延後降落，故答案為 b）To announce a landing delay due to bad weather。

# 4 - 2. 🎧

答案：a）All passengers are probably in their seats.（所有乘客都可能在座位上。）

中譯：以下何者正確描述飛機上的狀況？

　　　a）所有乘客都可能在座位上。

　　　b）電力被關掉了。

　　　c）所有的乘客都可能覺得困惑。

　　　d）空服員在走道上。

題解：文中提到 ...please note that the seat belt sign is now turned on. Please remain seated with your seat belts fastened,... 推知乘客應該都已經坐在位子上了，故答案為 a）All passengers are probably in their seats.

# 題解 9

## 1.

**答案**：b ) owing to（因為）

**中譯**：有些學生無法調整網頁版型以符合他們的需求，或許是因為缺乏使用網頁版型，或缺少練習，或科技技術本身的問題。

　　a ) 因為　　　　　　　b ) 因為　　　　　　c ) 幸好　　　　　d ) 到期的

**題解**：同樣是「因為」，because 後面要加 of 再加原因，owing to 可直接加原因，所以答案應是 b ) owing to（因為）。

## 2.

**答案**：d ) flourishing（繁榮、興旺）

**中譯**：1983 年 Peter Wold 創辦一個蓬勃發展的藝術社區；由於一群新世代有才華的藝術家、堅定支持的畫廊經營者以及一些文化機構的共同參與，這個社區生氣盎然。

　　a ) 逐漸衰敗的　　　b ) 有挑戰性的

　　c ) 互相競爭的　　　d ) 繁榮、興旺的

**題解**：由 talented young artists, committed gallery owners and cultural institutions 可推測這藝術社區應是蓬勃發展的，因此選 d ) flourishing（繁榮、興旺的）。

## 3.

**答案**：b）dividends（紅利）

**中譯**：由於疲弱的營運表現，Hobson 汽車公司的股東獲得的分紅寥寥可數。

　　a）轉移　　　　　　　　　　　b）紅利

　　c）占卜　　　　　　　　　　　d）部門

**題解**：由 shareholders 及 poor business showing 可推論獲利不佳應是指「紅利」。

## 4. 🎧

**聽力原文**：

In the past 20 years, interest in healthy food in America and Europe has grown tremendously. What began with a handful of people has grown to a significant portion of the population of many countries. A lot of this interest is in various traditional Japanese foods. Foods like miso, umeboshi and hijiki have become very popular because of their health benefits. This has opened a new market for Japanese food product companies which before only had the population of their island nation to sell to, but now can get a high price for their goods by exporting to the West.

**原文翻譯**：

過去 20 年來，歐美兩地對於健康飲食的興趣大幅提升。原本只是一小撮的人口，如今已在世界各國成長為顯著比例的人口。而當中有不少人對多樣化的日本傳統食品很有興趣。像味噌、梅干、鹿尾菜這類有益健康的食品日漸風行。這也為許多日本食品業業者打開新市場，以前只有其島國內的消費族群，如今則可以以高價外銷西方國家。

**答案：**d ) It has expanded greatly.（大幅的擴增）

**中譯：**過去 20 年來對於健康食品的興趣發生了何改變？

a ) 慢慢地減少。

b ) 幾乎保持原狀。

c ) 變得不被重視。

d ) 大幅的擴增。

**題解：**開頭 In the past 20 years, interest in healthy food in America and Europe has grown tremendously. 便可知道大眾對於健康飲食興趣大幅提升。

# 題解 10

## 1.

**答案**：d) outstanding（傑出的）

**中譯**：員工把低流動率歸功於 Boleyn 女士傑出的領導特質。

　　　a) 吉祥的　　　　　b) 聲名狼藉的　　　　c) 暴怒的　　　　d) 傑出的

**題解**：因是正向的歸功於 Boleyn 女士的領導，所以選項 d) outstanding（傑出的）最符合文意。

## 2.

**答案**：a) improvement（改善）

**中譯**：官員將服務的改善歸功於軟體升級，讓系統運作更流暢。

　　　a) 改善　　　　　b) 舉起　　　　　c) 增加　　　　　d) 移位

**題解**：因為軟體的升級，所以服務才能改善，因此選選項 a) improvement（改善）。

## 3.

**答案**：c) poor（差勁的）

**中譯**：多數的房屋建設公司把不理想的房市表現歸咎於不穩定的經濟和潛在客戶縮減的貸款。

　　　a) 有希望的　　　b) 很有可能的　　　c) 差勁的　　　d) 富啟發性的

題解：由後面的缺點：不穩定的經濟和潛在客戶縮減的貸款，可以推論出房市的表現應是
c) poor（差勁的）。

# 4 - 1. ～ 4 - 2.

聽力原文：

And now, a public radio safety announcement. With a recent rise in automobile accidents attributed to unsafe lane changes and with the holiday weekend approaching, the California Highway Safety Commission has issued the following reminder to all drivers. When changing lanes in your automobile, just remember the word smog, spelled S-M-O-G.

"S" is for signal; turn on your blinker so other cars can know your intentions. "M" is for mirrors; look in both your rearview and side mirrors to make sure the lanes are clear. "O" is for over; look over your shoulder to make extra sure the lanes are clear. When all of this is done, "G" is for go; go ahead and change lanes. After you have changed lanes, be sure to turn off your blinker and continue checking your mirrors for other cars.

原文翻譯：

現在是電台的公眾安全宣導時間。有鑑於最近因危險變換車道引起的汽車事故大增，加上週末假期將至，加州國道安全委員會提醒所有駕駛人：當要變換汽車車道時，記得 smog，S-M-O-G 這個字。

S 是方向燈；打開你的方向燈讓其他車輛知道你的意圖。M 是後照鏡；查看你的後視鏡和兩側的鏡子以確保車道淨空。O 代表回頭，回頭查看再度確認車道是否淨空。G 是行駛；檢查完畢後就可以變換車道。在變換車道後，確定已關掉你的方向燈並繼續檢視鏡子以留意其他車輛。

## 4 - 1.

**答案：** c ) A radio DJ（電台主持人）

**中譯：** 誰最可能提出這項建議？

    a ) 技工          b ) 學習駕駛者          c ) 電台主持人          d ) 汽車設計者

**題解：** 從第一句可得知這是電台的宣導內容，因此選項 c ) A radio DJ（電台主持人）最符合。

## 4 - 2.

**答案：** c ) When changing lanes（在變換車道時）

**中譯：** 駕駛人何時需要記得 "S-M-O-G"？

    a ) 在倒車時                          b ) 在泥濘的道路上時

    c ) 在變換車道時                     d ) 在停車時

**題解：** 文中不斷強調是 changing lanes in your automobile，所以選選項 c ) When changing lanes（在變換車道時）。

# 題解 11

## 1.

**答案**：c）Delays（延遲）

**中譯**：McWicky 公司延遲未繳的應收帳款高達九千萬，將會導致商業現金流量的縮減。

a）準時　　　　b）規律　　　　c）延遲　　　　d）防護

**題解**：文後提到現金流量會縮減，因此可推論出前面的公司收入應是被延遲了，所以是選項 c）Delays（延遲）最符合原意。

## 2.

**答案**：a）effective（有效的）

**中譯**：高度寫實的醫學模擬能夠補足病人照護教育的不足且帶來有效的學習。

a）有效的　　　　b）感情的　　　　c）選擇性的　　　　d）動機

**題解**：由 complement（補足）可以判斷出前面的 simulations（模擬）應是有正面幫助的，所以選有正面意向的 a）effective（有效的）。

## 3.

**答案**：c）treatment（治療）

**中譯**：密集的治療牙齦疾病可以改善血液循環，也能顯著降低身體的感染。

a ) 無知　　　　　b ) 運動　　　　　c ) 治療　　　　　　d ) 分類

題解：從 gum disease（牙齦疾病）可以判斷出相對應的字是 c ) treatment（治療）。

# 4 - 1. ～ 4 - 2.

聽力原文：

Now that your resume has gotten you an interview, it is time to form a plan of attack to make sure that you get what you want out of the exchange. While many interview advice resources say it is best to tell the interviewer what he or she wants to hear, that can often lead to getting a job that is not suited for you, which you will later regret.

Your answers at an interview should be absolutely truthful; however, it is good to phrase them strategically. This can be a test of your eloquence.

原文翻譯：

由於你的履歷已為你爭取到面試，該是時候擬訂作戰計畫，以確保你得到自己想要的。雖然很多面試建議你最好告訴主試官他們想聽的，但那通常會讓你得到不適合你的工作，而你會因此而後悔。

你在面試中所給的答案應該都要誠實，然而有技巧性的表達方式也很重要。這是測試你口才的機會。

# 4 -1. 🎧

答案：b ) Getting the greatest benefit from it（從中獲取最大利益）

中譯：依據上述的話題，在面試前應該要計畫什麼？

　　　a ) 在履歷上加添經驗　　　　　　b ) 從中獲取最大利益

　　　c ) 避開面試官　　　　　　　　　d ) 在面試中表現得很健談

**題解**：文中提到面試前 ...make sure that you get what you want out of the exchange.（確保得到自己最想要的），因此選項 b）Getting the greatest benefit from it.（從中獲取最大利益）最符合文意。

# 4 - 2. 🎧

**答案**：a）With only the truth（說實話）

**中譯**：依據上述的話題，面試者在回答問題時應如何？

a）說實話　　　　　　　　　　　　b）說任何自己想說的

c）說主試官想聽的話　　　　　　　d）回答「是」或「否」

**題解**：文末提到面試的答案應是 ...absolutely truthful...（完全誠實）所以是選項 a）With only the truth（說實話）最符合文意。

# 題解 12

## 1.

**答案**：c ) interruptions（中斷）

**中譯**：航空公司因經濟衰退而停飛某些航線的服務，或許能說明 2008 年旅客量減少的原因。

a ) 連接　　　　　b ) 干預　　　　　c ) 中斷　　　　　d ) 插曲

**題解**：從 stopped flying（停飛）和 decrease of the number（數量減少）可以判斷出航空業應是 c ) interruptions（中斷）航線服務。

## 2.

**答案**：d ) fatalities（死亡事故）

**中譯**：依據汽車安全中心的說法，每年的汽車死亡事故至少有 10% 起因於汽車的瑕疵。

a ) 失敗　　　　　b ) 肥料　　　　　c ) 布料　　　　　d ) 死亡事故

**題解**：從 Auto defects（汽車的瑕疵）和 Auto Safety（汽車安全）等字可判斷出空格應填汽車意外事故，所以選項 d ) fatalities（死亡事故）。

# 3.

**答案**：b) reductions（減少）

**中譯**：加熱用燃油的價格上漲或許能解釋近來營運資金的減少。

a) 衰退　　　　　　b) 減少　　　　　　c) 反彈　　　　　　d) 回絕

**題解**：從前面的油價上揚可以推斷出這樣額外的支出會造成資金縮減，所以是選項 b) reductions（減少）。

# 4 - 1. ～ 4 - 2.

**聽力原文**：

As regular viewers of *American Business Nightly* know, this week we have been featuring some of our country's most successful business executives. Tonight, we welcome Mark Holcomb, founder and marketing director of Holcomb Art Limited based in Englewood, Colorado. A self-trained graphic designer, he has shifted his artistic creativity from the computer screen to ceramic products. Along the way, Mr. Holcomb has rapidly developed his business from a four-person firm to a company that earned a pretax profit of over 19 million dollars last year alone. Mr. Holcomb, how do you explain your success?

**原文翻譯**：

一如《美國商業晚報》的忠實觀眾所知，我們本週推出國內最成功的商業主管特輯。今晚，我們邀請到 Mark Holcomb，他是在科羅拉多州的 Englewood 發跡的 Holcomb 藝術公司創建者兼行銷總監。他是自學的平面設計師，將本身的藝術創作從電腦螢幕延伸到陶瓷製品上。一路走來，Holcomb 先生快速地拓展生意，將一間只有四個人的公司發展到去年稅前盈餘超過 1900 萬的企業。Holcomb 先生，您如何解釋您的成功？

## 4 -1. 🎧 ........................................................................

**答案**：c ) It designs ceramic products.（設計陶瓷製品）

**中譯**：Holcomb 先生的公司從事什麼業務？

　　　　a ) 為網站設計圖像。　　　　　　　b ) 從事市場研究。

　　　　c ) 設計陶瓷製品。　　　　　　　　d ) 訓練陶瓷藝術家。

**題解**：文中提到他的創作 ...from the computer screen to ceramic products.，因此可得知是選項 c ) It designs ceramic products.（設計陶瓷製品。）

## 4 - 2. 🎧 ........................................................................

**答案**：a ) It developed over a short period.（在很短的時間內就迅速發展。）

**中譯**：關於 Holcomb 先生的公司，下列敘述何者為真？

　　　　a ) 在很短的時間內就迅速發展。　　b ) 改變了整個行業。

　　　　c ) 在新產品上投資了 1900 萬。　　d ) 在經濟上有困難。

**題解**：文末提到 ...has rapidly developed his business...，因此可以得知答案為 a ) It developed over a short period.（在很短的時間內就迅速發展）。

## 題解 13

### 1.

**答案**：b) unemployed（失業的）

**中譯**：已經有傳言到四樓，某些員工害怕因服務收入的減少，可能在聖誕節前遭到解雇。

　　a) 不滿的　　　　　　b) 失業的　　　　　c) 分類的　　　　　d) 未交代的

**題解**：從 fear（恐懼）和 service cutbacks（服務收入的減少）可推論出員工害怕的應是 b) unemployed（失業的）。

### 2.

**答案**：c) enter（進入）

**中譯**：使用你的飯店房卡方式是：只要將卡片插入門把上的細縫；當顯示燈由紅轉綠，你就能開門進入房間。

　　a) 離開　　　　　　b) 加入　　　　　c) 進入　　　　　d) 偷拿

**題解**：從文意得知，飯店房卡是為了讓房客能夠開門進入房間，所以選項 c) enter（進入）最符合文意。

### 3.

**答案**：d) prosperous（興旺的）

中譯：1990 年成立的 A & M 藝術公司，快速地興旺成長並成為國內最大的網站設計公司。
　　　a) 明顯的　　　　　b) 大膽的　　　　　c) 明顯的　　　　　d) 興旺的

題解：從 quickly grew（快速成長）和 became the largest web site design firm（成為最大的網站設計公司）可推論出該公司前景看好，所以選項 d) prosperous（興旺的）最符合文意。

# 4 - 1. ～ 4 - 2.

聽力原文：

Good morning. Glad to see you're all here. Mr. Sims and I have called this meeting to address the policies and your concerns over the changeover next month when we officially become a franchise in the Welton chain of stores. First of all, let us reassure you all that no jobs will be lost, nor will employees have hours cut. There will be a change in the dress code, however. Welton has a different policy about what you wear at work. Other than that, everything, including your medical coverage, will remain as it is today.

原文翻譯：

早安，很高興在這裡見到你們各位。我和 Sims 先生召開此次會議是為了說明公司的政策以及當我們下個月正式成為 Welton 連鎖店的特約經銷商後，你們對於經營權轉換的顧慮。首先，我們再次向你們保證沒有任何人會被解雇，也沒有任何員工會被縮減工時。然而服裝的規定會有所更動，Welton 對於工作有不同的服裝規定。除此之外，任何事情，包括你們的醫療保險，都將會維持現狀。

# 4 -1. 🎧

答案：d) It is being absorbed by another firm.（被另一家公司收購。）

中譯：公司的生意型態將會如何轉變？

　　　a) 它將在下個月關閉。　　　　　　b) 它將改變商品線。

　　　c) 要開展新的連鎖店。　　　　　　d) 被另一家公司收購。

題解：文中提到 ...officially become a franchise in the Welton chain of stores...（正式成為 Welton 公司的特約經銷商），因此可推論它是 d) It is being absorbed by another firm.（被另一家公司收購。）

# 4 - 2. 🎧 ............................................................

答案：c) Rules about clothing（服裝規定）

中譯：下個月將會有什麼改變？

　　　a) 醫療保險　　　　　　　　　　　b) 工作時數

　　　c) 服裝規定　　　　　　　　　　　d) 職位數量

題解：文中提到 ...will be a change in the dress code... 因此可得知改變的是 c) Rules about clothing（服裝規定）。

# 索引 Index 以下以句型關鍵字排列

## A

| | | |
|---|---|---|
| accept | B-8 | p. 82 |
| access to | C-7 | p. 102 |
| according to | A-1 | p. 46 |
| account for | D-12 | p. 138 |
| aim | D-4 | p. 122 |
| apologize | B-4 | p. 74 |
| appear | C-5 | p. 98 |
| approve | B-8 | p. 82 |
| as well as | C-10 | p. 108 |
| attend | B-10 | p. 86 |
| attribute | D-10 | p. 134 |
| award | A-10 | p. 64 |

## B

| | | |
|---|---|---|
| because of | D-9 | p. 132 |
| become | D-13 | p. 140 |

## C

| | | |
|---|---|---|
| certain | A-5 | p. 54 |
| charge | D-5 | p. 124 |
| claim | B-5 | p. 76 |
| (be) committed to | D-2 | p. 118 |
| communicate | B-1 | p. 68 |
| complaint | B-5 | p. 76 |
| connect | A-3 | p. 50 |
| contact | A-3 | p. 50 |

## D

| | | |
|---|---|---|
| describe | C-6 | p. 100 |
| due to | D-8 | p. 130 |

## E

| | | |
|---|---|---|
| ensure | A-6 | p. 56 |
| explain | D-12 | p. 138 |

## G

| | | |
|---|---|---|
| grow | D-13 | p. 140 |

## H

| | | |
|---|---|---|
| happen to | B-2 | p. 70 |

## I

| | | |
|---|---|---|
| in order to | D-3 | p. 120 |
| in place of | C-2 | p. 92 |
| instead of | C-2 | p. 92 |
| intention | D-4 | p. 122 |
| introduce | D-6 | p. 126 |

## J

| | | |
|---|---|---|
| join | B-10 | p. 86 |

## K

| | | |
|---|---|---|
| keep | C-1 | p. 90 |
| keep | D-7 | p. 128 |

## L

| | | |
|---|---|---|
| launch | D-6 | p. 126 |
| lawsuit | B-5 | p. 76 |
| lead to | D-11 | p. 136 |
| located (be) | A-8 | p. 60 |
| look | C-5 | p. 98 |

## N

| | | |
|---|---|---|
| negotiate | B-1 | p. 68 |

## O

| | | |
|---|---|---|
| occur to | B-2 | p. 70 |
| owing to | D-9 | p. 132 |

## P

| | | |
|---|---|---|
| participate in | B-10 | p. 86 |
| pity | B-3 | p. 72 |
| place ... under | C-8 | p. 104 |
| pleasure | B-3 | p. 72 |
| positive | A-5 | p. 54 |
| prevent | C-1 | p. 90 |
| provide | C-11 | p. 110 |
| purpose | D-4 | p. 122 |
| put ... under | C-8 | p. 104 |

## R

| | | |
|---|---|---|
| rather than | B-6 | p. 78 |
| reach | A-3 | p. 50 |
| recommend | B-9 | p. 84 |
| regard | C-6 | p. 100 |
| remain | D-7 | p. 128 |
| remind | A-4 | p. 52 |
| replace | C-3 | p. 94 |
| report | A-9 | p. 62 |
| result in | D-11 | p. 136 |

# S

| seem | C-5 | p. 98 |
|---|---|---|
| shame | B-3 | p. 72 |
| (be) situated | A-8 | p. 60 |
| start | D-6 | p. 126 |
| stay | D-7 | p. 128 |
| stop | C-1 | p. 90 |
| suggest | B-9 | p. 84 |
| (be) supposed to | A-7 | p. 58 |
| sure | A-5 | p. 54 |

# T

| thanks to | D-9 | p. 132 |
|---|---|---|
| There is a possibility | D-1 | p. 116 |
| There is no doubt | C-12 | p. 112 |
| There is no evidence | C-12 | p. 112 |
| There is no question | C-12 | p. 112 |
| treat | C-6 | p. 100 |
| turn | D-13 | p. 140 |

# U

| unless | C-9 | p. 106 |
|---|---|---|

# W

| whether | A-2 | p. 48 |
|---|---|---|
| would prefer to | B-7 | p. 80 |
| would rather | B-7 | p. 80 |

Linking English · 一生必學的測驗系列
# TOEIC 900（II）

2010年12月初版　　　　　　　　　　　　　　　定價：新臺幣330元
有著作權 · 翻印必究
Printed in Taiwan.

編　　者　陳　超　明
著　　者　Stephanie Morris
　　　　　及其工作團隊
發行人　林　載　爵

出　版　者　聯經出版事業股份有限公司　　　叢書主編　李　　　芃
地　　址　台北市基隆路一段180號4樓　　　校　　對　謝　一　秀
編輯部地址　台北市基隆路一段180號4樓　　　　　　　　李　靜　儀
叢書主編電話　(02)87876242轉226　　　　　　　　張　雅　芳
台北忠孝門市：台北市忠孝東路四段561號1樓　內文排版　江　宜　蔚
電　　話：(02)27683708　　　　封面設計　陳　皇　旭
台北新生門市：台北市新生南路三段94號　　　剪輯後製　純粹錄音
電　　話：(02)23620308　　　　　　　　後製有限公司
台中分公司：台中市健行路321號
暨門市電話：(04)22371234ext.5
高雄辦事處：高雄市成功一路363號2樓
電　　話：(07)2211234ext.5
郵政劃撥帳戶第0100559-3號
郵撥電話：27683708
印　刷　者　文鴻彩色製版印刷有限公司
總　經　銷　聯合發行股份有限公司
發　行　所：台北縣新店市寶橋路235巷6弄6號2樓
電　　話：(02)29178022

行政院新聞局出版事業登記證局版臺業字第0130號

本書如有缺頁，破損，倒裝請寄回聯經忠孝門市更換。　　ISBN　978-957-08-3726-1 (平裝)
聯經網址：www.linkingbooks.com.tw
電子信箱：linking@udngroup.com

國家圖書館出版品預行編目資料

TOEIC 900（Ⅱ）/陳超明主編．Stephanie
Morris及其工作團隊著．初版．臺北市．聯經．
2010年12月（民99年）．288面．18×20公分．
（Linking English・一生必學的測驗系列）
ISBN　978-957-08-3726-1（平裝）

1.多益測驗

805.1895　　　　　　　　　　　　　99019410

# TOEIC Career

## 多益職場產業排行榜

外派
海外幹部
**750分**

部門經理
**700分**

儲備幹部
**650分**

新進人員
**500分**

ETS. TOEIC.

多益 ▸ 幫助企業

『將對的人放在對的位置上』

| 產業別 排名 | TOEIC及**十大產業**與 工作機會連結需求排名 |
|---|---|
| ① | 文教相關業 |
| ② | 電子資訊相關業 |
| ③ | 大眾傳播相關業 |
| ④ | 一般製造業 |
| ⑤ | 政治宗教及社福相關業 |
| ⑥ | 法律／會計／顧問／研發業 |
| ⑦ | 批發及零售業 |
| ⑧ | 旅遊／休閒／運動業 |
| ⑨ | 建築營造及不動產相關業 |
| ⑩ | 金融投顧及保險業 |

| 產業別 排名 | TOEIC及**十大職務**與 工作機會連結需求排名 |
|---|---|
| ① | 文字工作類 |
| ② | 學術／教育／輔導類 |
| ③ | 行銷／企劃／專案管理類 |
| ④ | 行政／法務類 |
| ⑤ | 經營／人資類 |
| ⑥ | 客服／業務／貿易類 |
| ⑦ | 研發相關類 |
| ⑧ | 資材／運輸類 |
| ⑨ | 生產製造／品管類 |
| ⑩ | 資訊軟體系統類 |

▸ 資料來源:104人力銀行

### 更多企業多益相關職缺

日月光半導體・友訊科技・中強光電・中國信託・GARMIN・HTC・英業達・技嘉科技・金寶電子・LG CHEM(TAIWAN)・Microsoft・長榮航空・茂迪・南亞電路板・太金寶電通・泰興工程・國瑞汽車(TOYOTA製造商)・統一超商・裕隆日產・復興航空・第一銀行・勤業眾信・億光電子・寶成工業

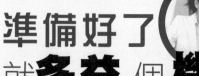

準備好了
就**多益**個**機會**

請上網站: **www.toeic.com.tw**